A Princess's Sword

Sarah Beiler

A Princess's Sword – by Sarah Beiler

Published in the United States.

Editor – Lydia Huth, Kelsey Beiler
Book Cover – ebooklaunch.com
Map Design – Leah Aamot
Book Format – Rachel Beiler
Publishing Consultant – Adrian Essigmann
Project Director – Evonne Beiler
First publication 2020

This book was published in memory of Sarah Beiler

She was involved in a horse riding accident and left this earth to be with Jesus at age 17. This work appears as we found it in the middle of edits….

The Alderian Kingdom Series

A Princess's Sword

A King's Death

A Queen's Quest

A Prince's Revenge

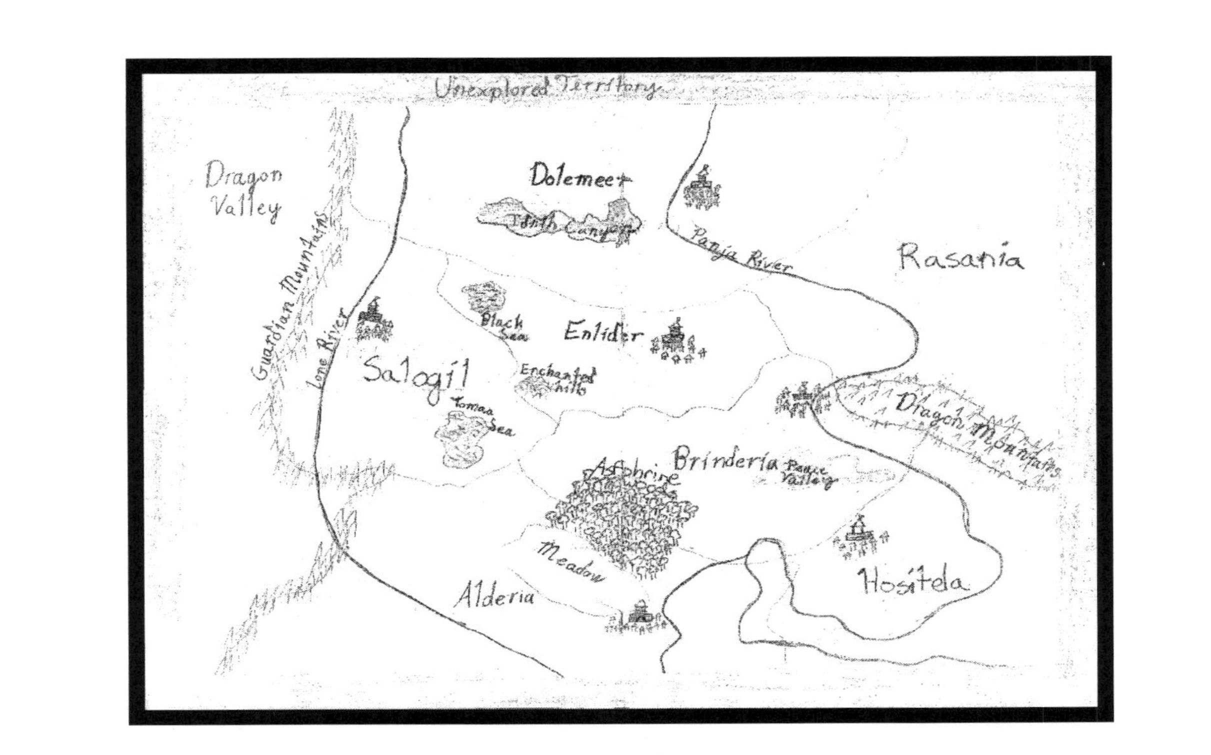
Unexplored Territory
Dragon Valley
Dolemeet
Guardian Mountains
Lone River
Panja River
Rasania
Black Sea
Enlider
Salogil
Enchanted hills
Tomaa Sea
Dragon Mountains
Brinderia
Peace Valley
Meadow
Alderia
Hositela

Once upon a time,
there lived a
princess...

Chapter One

"Princess Arilina!"

"Yes?" I replied, sitting straight up in bed. The door swung open into my room, letting in a breath of air that disturbed the tapestries decorating the wall.

A young maid rushed in, tears making tracks down her frightened face. "Hurry! There is a flying Erif dragon at the castle's north side! It is burning the barracks! What are we going to do?"

As she started to sob, I realized I needed to take control. I bent down beside her and placed a comforting arm around her shoulders. "Stay here," I commanded and then quickly grabbed my cloak and sword.

She nodded her head and choked out, "But where are you going?"

"Do not worry about me. I will be fine. Do not come out until I return, understand?" Biting her lip, she nodded. As I left my room, I thought of a plan. *The barracks, hmm?* I would have to hurry!

Five minutes later, I reached the bottom of the castle. I opened the door and stepped out into the chilly night air. With my hand resting on one of my small throwing daggers, I glanced around me, then hurried across the courtyard to the barracks.

Flames leaped into the dark sky. The fire was throwing enough light that I could see the people running toward it with buckets. Several knights were firing arrows at a dragon spewing fire. It was on the ground, but I caught a glimpse of wings folded up on its back. I drew my sword and stepped closer to it, staying in the safety of the stone buildings.

I analyzed the dragon. It was the size of a small horse. It took a while to remember my training, but then, in the midst of the chaos, it came to me. If it was the size of a horse, that meant it could shoot flames ten feet forward and two and a half feet wide.

When I was thirty yards away, I prepared to close the distance. I took a deep breath then jerked as I felt a hand on my shoulder. When I spun around, I saw Father's face inches from mine.

“Arilina, what are you doing?”

"Father! Why are you here?"

"You cannot take on an Erif dragon with a sword, you know that!"

"I could have done it! It would have worked!"

"How? You could have been shot by our own archers!"

"But Father!"

"I have enough problems with this dragon without adding my stubborn daughter to them."

Chastised, I hung my head. "My apologies."

"Go back to your room, quickly now."

"But what about the fire?"

"There are enough people here. Please go, Arilina." I hesitated, then nodded and turned back to the Keep. After hurrying up the stairs to my room, I found the trembling maid.

"What is happening, Princess Arilina?" she asked.

"Everything is fine. The knights are taking care of the dragon and the servants are stopping the fire."

"Oh, good." She breathed a sigh of relief and recovered her composure. "I am afraid I overreacted. My sincerest apologies. Is there anything I can get for you, your highness?" My heart went out to the girl, who was only eleven or twelve. Despite being four or five years younger than me and terrified, she still continued to serve me.

I smiled at her. "No, that is fine, thank you."

"Of course, your highness." She curtsied and hurried out of the room. I threw myself on my bed. Out of habit, my eyes traced the golden swirls that were stitched across the bottom of the blue tapestries around my room.

Why had I not been faster? I sighed. Father was right; I most likely would have gotten hurt by our own archers. I needed to think before throwing myself headlong into problems. *Just think, Arilina.* I fell asleep lecturing myself.

When I woke up the next morning, I rushed to get up and change my clothes. Then I began to mentally prepare myself for the rebuke I was going to get from my father.

Ten minutes later, a maid opened the door and said, "Your highness?"

"Yes?" I replied, looking up from the book I was reading.

"His majesty, your father, wants you to meet him at the stables in fifteen minutes."

"Thank you, you are dismissed." After standing, I walked over to the bookshelf and placed the book back in its proper spot. I threw my deep blue cloak around me and made my way to the stables, dreading the talk I was going to have with Father.

As I stepped through the stable door, I was greeted by whinnying. My mare, Leilia, neighed an extra greeting for me. I walked over to her stall and opened the top part of the door. She thrust her head out of her stall then pricked her ears like she did when she noticed something. I spun around and saw Father approaching.

"Hello, Father."

"Arilina, do you think what you did last night was smart?" His voice, though firm, was gentle. He was not the type of man to get angry and shout, but when he scolded me like this, I felt deep shame because I had disappointed him so.

"No, it was not. I was not thinking."

A soft smile came over his lips. "I am glad you realize that." He closed his eyes for a moment, then opened them. "Your life is so precious to me, and I would have great sorrow if you were hurt or killed foolishly. I hope you understand that the consequences of your actions do not just affect you, but also the others around you."

"I understand. I do regret it."

"Good. Now there is another reason I called you here. We have worked on throwing daggers, which you excel at, and we have covered sword fighting. But in all your training, I failed to give you a bow. Do not think that this is a reward for your behavior last night. The truth of the matter is, I was already planning on giving it to you today. Consider this a reward for the effort you have put into sword fighting. Even though at times it was difficult, you remained diligent through it all." He retrieved a bow and a quiver full of arrows from a cabinet nearby.

The bow was beautiful! It was made from yew wood, so it was brown—almost orange—in color. The grain ran in straight lines and was sanded to a smooth finish. The arrows were crafted out of the exotic rosewood tree. At the end of each arrow, the stabilizing feathers were dyed a light brown. To distinguish it from the rest, the index feather had a faint red zigzag pattern.

My eyes were drawn back to the bow. Paintings decorated the limbs, and I studied one end. It had a sword, a bow with an arrow on its string, and a chainmail shirt. I inspected the other limb. This one showed flowers, an elegant dress, and a needle pulling thread through fabric.

I was baffled for a moment; but then I laughed. “Oh! One limb shows what Mother wants me to be, and the other one shows what you want me to be.” Father nodded and pointed to the handle. I looked at it and let out another laugh. The carving was a bow shooting a flower, a chainmail dress, and a sword pulling thread through some fabric.

“And that,” I said, pointing at the handle, “is what will happen if I try to please both of you!”

Father smiled and started to walk toward the door. He called over his shoulder, “Come, we will soon see if you enjoy shooting it as much as you enjoy looking at it."

I followed Father to the archery range where his knights practiced shooting. I pulled back the bow, aimed and shot. It was high and a little to the left. Some knights were practicing there as well. Little by little, they all began to gather around me and there were a few soft murmurs among them. I tried to concentrate as best I could, but finally, I could not focus anymore.

I turned to face them and asked, "Is there something I can help you with?"

One of them stepped forward and said, "I apologize if we are distracting to you; it was not our intention to be rude. My men and I were wondering..." He cleared his throat. "Well, your highness, is this the first time you have ever shot?"

"Yes, why?"

"Milady, I have never seen any with your talent."

"Talent?"

"Yes! Some people take years to finally learn the proper form. But you have already mastered resting the arrow consistently on the same anchor spot."

"Consistent? Look at that target. My arrows are not even close to being together," I protested.

"That is only because you are not strong enough yet. With more time and practice, the muscles needed to hold the bow at full draw will strengthen. Soon you will be able to hold it steady; then you will be able to hit the target exactly where you want. But we will bother you no longer. Good day, your highness."

"Good day." I tried to understand what they had just said. *I had talent?*

Chapter Two

The next morning my arms were sore from my shooting. At breakfast, I winced when one of my muscles protested at a movement.

Mother noticed and asked, "What have you been doing, dear?"

Before I could reply, Father distracted her by saying, "Arilina, have I ever told you the story of how your mother and I met?"

I shook my head. A smile crossed my mother's face. "I do not think I will ever forget that day."

Father gazed at her fondly. "Do you wish to tell it, dear, or shall I?"

"You can tell it, but I will interject if you forget anything."

So, Father began his story. "Twenty years ago, I was a twenty-one-year-old prince."

"A handsome prince," Mother added with a smile.

"Yes, well, it was during that year I went to Dolameer to meet the allies I would have when I was king. There, I met a black-haired beauty of a princess. A gem among stones." Mother blushed. "For six months, I courted her as was custom and we were married soon after."

Mother protested, "How quickly you skip over one of the most horrible days of my life!"

I shot a confused look at my parents. "I do not understand. I thought you wanted to be engaged. Why do you say it was horrible?" I asked.

Father sighed and looked at his wife. "Do you want to tell it, my dear?"

"I do. Arilina, your father was the dashing, blond-haired, blue-eyed prince in every girl's dreams. Before I ever met him, I had heard about him and longed to meet him. One day, my mother told me that he was coming. I was beyond excited. The day drew closer and closer. When it arrived, I was ready. I had prepared for this moment, it seemed, my entire life. I entered the room, and we both stopped as we caught sight of each other. It seemed like we were the only two in the room. Then the Lady Revaila arrived."

"I had quite forgotten her," Father said.

"Well, I had not. She had always been a thorn in my side—the bane of my existence, you might say. She acted as though she were superior to me, and I, a princess! Her one pleasure in life, it seemed, was to make me miserable. She treated me like I was a child of thirteen instead of my eighteen years. She herself was twenty-two. My one consolation was that she had yet to find a husband, but that day it appeared that all that would change. Your father seemed to be smitten with her."

Father leaned over and whispered in my ear, "I did it to make her jealous, of course."

Mother did not show she had heard but said, "He made a fool of himself over her. I had just about made up my mind that if a man could be that infatuated with Revaila, then he was not the man I had thought he was. In truth, I was trying my best not to cry. The whole evening had slipped from my control.

Then, someone was standing beside me. It was him. He asked me if I was enjoying the ball. He was more of a fool than I had thought. Anyone could have seen my unhappiness. I decided that if he was going to be foolish, I might as well be full of folly too. I told him I was having a marvelous time and that I had met a wonderful man. His eyes twinkled. He thought I was talking about him!"

Father interjected, "I really did, you know. But with her next words, my hopes were crushed. She said the name of Prince Celarin. She went on to describe him in glowing terms."

Mother continued the story. "It was my pride. I see that now. I was determined that this man would not know how miserable he was making me. I did feel something when I saw he was disappointed by my words. I did not think I felt regret, but triumph. At that moment, Celarin himself came and asked to dance. I agreed only to keep up my charade. I must be honest, though, Celarin was a dull man. He spoke of the things that interested him, never asking me of my opinion."

Father interrupted again. "I watched her dance. She appeared to be having a marvelous time. I tried to forget her, so I returned to the attention of Revaila."

"The night continued on as such for some time. Then the ball was over and I went to my room. But I could not sleep. I wandered into the gardens and sat on a bench. It was not long before I was crying. Everything had gone wrong. Then the bench creaked as someone sat beside me! I knew without looking that it was this prince from Alderia. It was just my fortune for this to happen. I ignored him."

"I did not know what to say to comfort this exquisite, crying creature. So we sat in silence. Then I apologized for trying to get her attention through jealousy."

"*You* apologized? I do not think so. It was *I* who apologized first."

"Then you force me to say you are wrong." They looked at each other across the table.

Mother cleared her throat. "We sat there in silence. Finally, I decided that I had nothing to lose, that this man had already seen me at the worst. So, I straightened, gathered my resolve, and apologized. He handed me a rose he plucked from beside us. I twirled it in my fingers, both of us pondering what my apology meant. Then, he too apologized for the way he had acted." Mother paused.

Father looked to the side. "Uh, yes, now that you say it... I believe that is how it happened after all." I hid a grin at Father's sheepish expression.

Mother smiled and continued, "We started the next day as if the first had never happened. It was only two weeks later that we both realized we were hopelessly in love. My father believed that two weeks was too short a time to truly know if we loved each other. He was determined that I would be happy in my marriage. His own union with my mother had not been the best, I regret to say. So, for six months, your father courted me."

"It was not my most flattering time of life, I must admit."

"Whatever are you talking about? It was a glorious time!"

"But I made a fool of myself; I even tried to write poetry!"

Mother flashed him a mischievous smile. "I still have that, you know."

Father stared at her. "You cannot be serious."

"I am. In fact, I memorized it."

Father's face held mock horror. "No!"

"Yes. Remember? It began like this:

As the sky needs the sun,
My dear, you are my only one."

Father's mock fright was becoming real. He jumped to his feet. "Go now, Arilina! While you still can!"

I laughed and slipped away from them. They probably wanted time alone together to relive the olden days.

I made my way down to the stables and visited Leilia. I sighed. Sometimes, it was fun to think that I could defend myself. Sometimes, I wondered if the need did arise, could I protect myself? Other times, I got tired of carrying my weaponry everywhere. It always had to be concealed too because it was not proper for a lady to have so many weapons. This was not too hard since Mother insisted I wear my cloak even with the slightest chill in the air, both inside and outside.

My cloak hid my sword and six throwing knives. I could keep my dagger in plain sight since ladies were supposed to appear experienced with a dagger. I was the only lady I knew who actually was an expert with the dagger though. I also kept a small throwing blade on the inside of my boot. This was by far my favorite weapon. I dubbed it my “boot blade”, although it was not a different weapon from a throwing knife. Its handle stuck out about half an inch above the top of my boot, so I could pull it out with speed to throw it.

I went over to the cabinet where my bow was stored and pulled the quiver and bow out together. I attached the quiver to my sword belt and swept my cloak over it, making it invisible. I debated where I could conceal the bow on my body when I glimpsed a stranger at the end of the stable. After I had placed the bow back in its hiding spot in the cabinet, I followed the man. I just spotted part of him rounding the far corner.

A moment later I caught up with him and asked, "What is your business in the royal stables of Alderia, sir?"

The stranger spun around at my voice, looking a bit angry. But when he discovered that I was a girl, a smile smoothed his features. "Well, fair lady, I am a humble merchant who is here to pick up some of these lovely horses."

My smile faded. Father always informed me about sales of our animals. He said it was because I needed to be familiar with the sales and transactions. So, I knew we were not selling any more horses this year.

He gave me a strange look, so I relaxed and said, "Well, I suppose I could show you some of the horses we might sell. What is your name?"

"Miryant. But do you not think a groom would have a better idea of what horses are available to buy?"

I blinked, my mind whirling, then blurted out the first thing that came to mind, "Um, I am the daughter of a groom."

"Really?" One of his eyebrows arched. I plastered a fake smile on my face and nodded while berating myself mentally. *A daughter of a groom?* With the dress I was wearing, there was not a chance he would believe me.

I gathered myself and said, “So, if you will follow me, I will show you some horses.”

“I think it would be better if I talked with your....” He paused then finished, “father.”

“Uh, I will show you a horse, and while you are looking at it, I will fetch my father.”

“Very well.” I took him three rows over and showed him a horse. Keeping the man in sight as long as I could, I called to a groom who was passing by, “Can you come here, please?”

He nodded and approached me, “What do you need, your royal—”

“Shh!” I held my finger to my lips.

He looked confused, “What is—?”

But I ignored him and whispered instructions to him. “Tell my father to come here immediately with ten or so guards!”

He nodded. “Of course, anything else?”

"No, just go!" After watching the groom disappear, I hurried back to the stranger.

"Ah, you are back, is your father coming?"

"Yes, uh, he will be here soon. What do you think of the mare?"

"Hmm. She has promise, but her back has a slight sway in it; is she old?"

"She is seven years old and has produced four foals."

"That explains it. Do you still have any of her foals?"

My mind scrambled for information about the horse. "Uh, two, I believe, both geldings. They are used in the cavalry." He nodded and looked over the mare. Just then, I glimpsed Father and some guards at the far end of the aisle.

"Sir, I need you to come with me."

"Where?"

"To the king. Your story does not make sense, and I believe you are lying."

"Oh?" He did not seem worried at all.

I tried to sound confident as I replied, "Yes. Father…now!" Father and his guards surrounded the man. He started questioning the man thoroughly, and I became more confused. The man had no fear and spoke with confidence. I had been certain he was lying, but now I was not so sure.

Father finally decided to assign two knights to go with him back to his country. He declared that Miryant should not return to Alderia for the time of one year. But I could not help but wonder—what had his true purpose really been?

Chapter Three

Months passed and I became a skilled archer both on the ground and on horseback. I could ride Leilia bareback and without any reins, while I shot from her back at a walk. Father was so proud of me. I must admit, I was prideful myself. Many of Father's knights were astonished at how fast I was developing my skills. But there were a few who said they had known all along that I would become an excellent archer.

I turned my focus back on the book I was reading. It was about dragons' strengths and weaknesses. I read the next entry; it was about Fika, a black dragon about the size of an adult sheep. They had sharp teeth and claws and could run as fast as a horse, but they did not have any wings. Their weakest point was exactly between their eyes. Usually, they were in groups of at least twenty-five and averaged around a hundred in a pack. The main reason we encountered them was that they attacked our livestock. They focused on younger animals like foals, calves, lambs and such.

The next entry was about Fire Dragons, usually referred to as Erif. It was long because Erif came in different sizes, and their ability to shoot flames varied. An Erif the size of a cat could shoot flames two feet forward and five inches wide. One the size of an adult cow could shoot flames eight feet forward and two feet wide. Their bodies were always flame-colored. Erif were only killed with a well-aimed arrow through one of their small eyes. Their main motivation was gold. They craved it and would do anything to get it in any form. There were times, though, when they would attack a person or village for no apparent reason. There was a subspecies of Erif dragons that could fly.

The entry after that was about Leahid. They were impossible to kill with the bow. They could fly and were very agile. Not only that, they were also incredibly durable. They were known to ambush people who were alone. If they bit someone, it was only a matter of time before that person died. Their poison was not only in their fangs but in their claws as well. People tried to avoid them at all costs since the only way to kill them was to engage them with a sword at close range. One more thing was interesting about the Leahid: they never attacked animals.

I flipped the page, but I never started reading it because bells began to ring—dragon attack!

My weapons ready, I rushed into the courtyard. It was jammed with people. The women and children were trying to get out of the way so the men could protect the livestock. Most of them were headed toward the village horse pastures, as that was our most valuable resource.

A man bumped into me. "My apologies, your highness."

He turned to go, but I grabbed his arm. "Wait! What is attacking?"

"Fika, your highness." He disappeared into the rest of the crowd. I joined the chaotic flow of people for a different reason: the stables were in that direction and so was Leilia. Not taking the time to saddle her, I slipped a bridle on her and swung onto her back. Soon, we were racing out of the castle into the surrounding village.

I was hoping no one would recognize me and say something to my mother since no one, aside from a few knights, was supposed to know of my fighting talent. Because of that, I chose to defend a remote sheep pasture. The shepherd was nowhere in sight and the sheep milled aimlessly without their leader.

A high-pitched bleat to my right caught my attention. Following the sound, I spotted a Fika carrying away a dead lamb in its mouth. It dropped with my arrow between its eyes. As I continued to ride, I found another dragon. I pulled back and felt the feather against my cheek. I released the bowstring but jerked at the last second when the thing snarled at me. The arrow sailed over the Fika's head. I pulled another arrow from my quiver and, this time held it steady. The arrow plunged into the dragon's head, killing it in a flash.

I rode Leilia around the pasture, killing the dragons. I missed three more times on my first shots, but the second arrows all found their marks. When I finally settled into a rhythm, it seemed too easy; just pick an arrow, nock it, pull the bow back, and aim.

That is when I reached for an arrow and found an empty quiver. So much for this being easy. I stopped Leilia. I could not pull the arrows out of the bodies because my tips were barbed. If I could manage to remove them I would damage them too much. I could go back to the castle and get more but that would also take some time. I focused back on the field; we were surrounded by dragons! While I had been lost in thought, the Fika had chosen their prey.

Counting them, I realized that seven formed a moving circle around me. I slid to the ground and threw a knife. Hitting my mark, I spun, throwing another. After I took out two more, I vaulted onto Leilia's back and slid down the other side. I hurled another blade, killing another dragon. I used my last knife then, but instead of hitting the next Fika between the eyes, it hit its nose. This dragon had been smart enough to jerk its head up and out of the way. It shook its head and the knife flew out, the tip badly bent. I reached down for my boot knife and released it out of my hand, killing the last unwounded Fika.

Drawing my sword, I engaged the injured one. It charged me, and I sidestepped. It turned its back to me and focused on my horse. Leilia backed away from the creature, tossing her head and snorting. I rushed from behind it and slammed my sword into the back of its neck. A spasm of pain ran through it, but it was not a fatal stroke. It wheeled to face me. Since it was slowed down by the pain, I managed to thrust my sword into its head.

I only had my sword and my dagger left. The book had said that arrows were the best defense against this particular dragon. Only if you were a skilled swordsman should you challenge a healthy Fika. I scanned my surroundings. Not seeing any living dragons, I cantered back to the castle, keeping an eye out for more Fika. I spied several more. I used my dagger to kill one, but the rest seemed to be retreating. I avoided them.

Since I felt strange without most of my weapons, I kept my hand on my sword. When we reached the stable, I slide off Leilia.

After making sure that she did not have any scrapes or cuts, I locked her in her stall. I straightened my skirt and arranged my cloak around my sword and empty quiver. I hurried to my room and tidied myself up as best I could. My dress was ruined, but it did not make any difference to me unless Mother caught sight of it.

Before I left, I took five books off the shelf and pulled out a box that had been concealed. I opened it up and picked out six shining throwing blades. They were light, but they could do some damage. Each one had an AE on it for Arilina Eral. All of my weapons had these letters on them. My sword, boot knife, and dagger all had it engraved on the hilt. My arrows had it on their index feathers, my bow had it on the handle, and my quiver bore the AE on its bottom. I put the box back and replaced the books.

I made my way downstairs and into the entrance room. My father was there with another man who appeared to be a knight. He was probably reporting on the attack. As I walked by, Father nodded at me and the man bowed. I dipped my head to acknowledge the bow. After exiting the room to avoid eavesdropping, I found myself in the evening room, aptly named since it was where we usually spent our evenings. Feeling weary, I sat down on a couch. Just as the thought of lying down on the couch and falling asleep seemed irresistible, Father entered the room.

"Well, Arilina, something interesting has happened."

"What?" I asked, still feeling tired.

"It seems someone single-handedly defended the sheep pasture. Thanks to this person we only lost three lambs." I wanted to protest. I had taken on a good deal of the dragons too, but I remained silent to avoid sounding prideful. Father continued, "This person killed twenty-seven Fika. The individual used three different weapons: a dagger, arrows and throwing knives." As he finished, he laid out a throwing blade and the top part of an arrow.

"But these are mine," I whispered, wide awake now, shocked at what Father was suggesting.

"But I certainly didn't kill twenty-seven…" I argued.

"Mmm, well I will show you just how you did it. First off, you had two dozen arrows in your quiver, and now it is empty. Out of twenty-four arrows, twenty killed Fika. Your dagger killed one and six out of seven of your throwing knives hit their mark. So, with your dagger, and throwing blades, you killed a total of seven. Then, with your twenty arrows that comes to twenty-seven."

It sank in then, and I thought of something. "No, I did not kill twenty-seven Fika," I contradicted again.

"Arilina, I just showed you—"

"I killed twenty-eight!"

"Twenty-eight? But how?" Father questioned.

"You will notice that the tip of the throwing dagger on the table is bent. It became that way after it hit the tough skull of a Fika. But I still killed that one with my sword."

"Twenty-eight! Arilina, I can't tell you how proud I am of you."

"So proud that you will replace my arrows for me?" I asked hopefully.

"Yes." He laughed. "Yes, we can go to the craftsman tomorrow afternoon."

"Sounds great to me. So, do you know how many Fika did attack?"

"So far we've found around two hundred dragon bodies; there must have been two packs."

"That is interesting. I would love to figure it all out, but right now I am exhausted. If anyone needs me, I will be in my room sleeping."

⌂⌂⌂

The moon shone down on a man staring into a dying fire in a nearby wood. He had seen the girl fight the Fika. She was good. It would make his job tougher. But he figured she would be too scared to actually harm a person, which gave him a good chance of fulfilling his task. That girl might be great at fighting, but he was better by far. An owl hooted behind him. Without a backward glance, he whipped out a knife and threw it over his shoulder. An instant later, the sound

of something hitting the ground followed.
Miryant smiled.

Chapter Four

I yawned and stretched. Noting the position of the sun, I realized that it was late morning. Exhausted from the fight and the mental strength I had used the previous day, I had slept longer to regain what I had lost.

When I reached the dining room, I discovered that only one place was set. I sat down and began to eat. My parents would have already eaten. Mother was probably thinking up some new menu for an upcoming feast and decorations for the dining hall. When there was no celebration, the long wooden table that ran the length of the room to my left lay empty. From the small ornate table where I ate, I could see the bright-colored tapestries that hung on the walls. Depicted on the cloth were past victories and fights. In one corner was an ancient one, close to three hundred years old. A knight had slain a dragon and a fair maiden fluttered her handkerchief. To honor the brave warrior, a king was there as well. With a sigh, I pushed away from the table, wondering where Father could be.

First, I went to the throne room. I concluded that the best place to search for him was the stables. I made my way through the stalls. Drifting down the rows of horses, I stroked their soft noses. Reaching Father's horse's stall, I found it empty. I ran my fingers over the smooth wood, touching the golden nameplate that read *Eriyc*. My gaze wandered across the aisle and rested on Leilia.

My eyes brightened. I could take Leilia on a ride! Looking out one of the stable's big windows, I saw something moving. I squinted trying to determine what it was. As my eyes focused, I realized it was a man dressed in black. He was in the shadow of a large oak. Arming myself with my bow and quiver full of new arrows, I rode out to see who was in the Asfohrine forest.

After riding across the meadow, I tied Leilia to a tree. I slipped into the forest. Smelling smoke, I approached a clearing, hiding behind trees. A smoldering fire lay in the middle of it. The aroma of stew wafted on a small breeze. Feeling something was wrong,

I turned to head back to Leilia. On turning, I was confronted by a sword, inches away from my face. My hand inched to my hilt.

"None of that!" he said, hitting my hand with the flat of his sword.

"Ouch!" He had not drawn blood, but my hand stung.

"Come with me and you will not get hurt. But if you try to put up a fight and make noise, well, it will be the last sound you make, understand?"

Alarmed, I nodded and asked, "What do you want with me?"

"I guess that is my little secret." He caught both my wrists, tying them with a rope he had pulled from a pocket.

"Wait a bit, I know you! You are the man who was in the stables a while ago. Miryant!"

"You are observant. It is true; you did catch me in the stables. That day I realized that you had a couple of surprises up your sleeve. But I too have many tricks of which you are unaware."

"But how did you get here? I mean, how did you escape from the knights? They are trained warriors."

"Well, they ran into a bit of bad luck when they were assigned to me. I am afraid that they are dead now."

My mind whirled. *Dead?* The sound of my breathing filled my ears. Out of nowhere tiny black spots began to dance in my vision. I pushed away the faintness that beckoned me.

Not noticing my shock, he continued. "Hmm, let me think, would you have walked or ridden a horse here? You rode your horse most likely and probably tied it at the edge of the woods. Yes, well, we cannot leave your horse tied up, can we?"

I stared at him, amazed at how he had figured that out without me saying a word. After he tied my hands together, we retraced my steps back to Leilia. He untied my horse then mounted her himself. He looked down at me, his mouth twitching at my outrage. "Well, come on now. We have to get started."

"Where are we going?"

He looked at me. "Do you honestly think I am going to tell you?"

I did not reply and followed him back to his campsite, fuming that he would dare ride my horse while I walked. Then I realized I had bigger problems on which to focus my emotions.

He dismounted, went over to a thicket, and soon returned leading another horse. He took my reins and tied them to his saddle. With some help from Miryant, I mounted, then he swung into his saddle and we headed off into the woods.

After some difficult riding, we came to a clearing and stopped. He pulled me out of the saddle, tied my ankles together, then pushed me to the ground. He lit a big fire and I managed to make my way over to it and warm myself. I soon grew sleepy, but my hunger kept me awake. I pushed myself into a sitting position and glared across the fire at my captor. He was eating bread and meat and appeared to be enjoying himself. My mouth screaming for water, I watched as he let precious drops of water fall to the ground without a care.

"No gentleman would dare to be so rude as to eat and drink in front of a starving lady," I complained.

"Oh, I do not think you are starving, Princess," he replied in a mild tone.

I gasped at his blatant rudeness, "Why, you—!"

"Fine, since you've pricked my conscience, you may have some of my bread." When he was done speaking, he tossed me a slice of bread and a container of water.

I grabbed the water clumsily with my bound hands, drank my fill, then muttered, "As if you have a conscience."

Almost as if appearing out of thin air, Miryant stood over me. "Did you say something about not liking my bread?" I vigorously shook my head and took a bite of the bread, spitting out the dirt that had mixed with it. The food eased my hunger somewhat and I soon was able to fall asleep.

The next morning, I woke up stiff and sore. I moaned as I pushed myself up to a sitting position. The man slumbered on the other side of the now-dying fire. My mouth was dry and demanded water. I wiggled my fingers, realizing that the rope had loosened overnight. I twisted my wrists. The rope was rough and it chafed, but I gritted my teeth and continued to turn my wrists and move my fingers.

Finally, I jerked my right hand out, and, reaching into my boot, I grabbed the concealed knife that was still there thankfully. I slashed the rope in half and unraveled it from my left hand then reached down and cut the rope that bound my ankles. I stayed sitting for a while moving my hands and feet to get the blood circulating again.

I stood up and crept over to Leilia, grabbing my weapons as I went, and scrambled onto her back. I did not dare to try to find the bridle, so I steered her with my knees away from the camp. After only a few paces, a twig snapped. Miryant sprang to his feet, instantly taking in the scene. I dug my heels into Leilia and she lunged into a run.

Behind me, I could hear a crashing noise and I realized Miryant was pursuing me. But I knew these woods well. Secret paths and hidden routes had all been discovered as I had explored this forest as a child. I had been watching the sun yesterday and had thought we had gone in a north-east direction. The fastest way back to the castle would be to go west then turn south. That would be what Miryant expected me to do, so I turned south and plunged off the path.

But we had barely gone two miles when disaster struck. We were walking, to give Leilia a little break, when the sun dimmed like a cloud had passed over it. Looking up, I glimpsed a scaly red tail disappearing behind the treetops. Erif dragon! I only hoped it had not singled me out for its prey.

Urging Leilia into a run, I looked back and stared in horror at a fire that was sweeping toward me. Leilia snorted with fear and pinned her ears to her head. Feeling her nervousness, I tried to calm her. But then a dragon, twice the size of my horse, landed in front of us.

Scared out of her wits, Leilia reared. Everything slowed down as I desperately tried to grab her mane but tumbled off her back. Panicked, she raced away into the woods. The

Erif dragon stalked closer to me. Gathering every last particle of strength, I rose to my feet. I drew back my bow and plunged an arrow into the eye of the dragon. It roared and I backed away from it. It spread its wings and took off, but it did not clear the trees. Plunging to and fro, it breathed fire in spurts. Fearing the danger of fire, I fled to a stream. As I hurried into the water, I slipped on a wet rock and my head hit the ground. Blackness descended around me.

⩩⩩⩩

Black trees. Charred grass. Gray sky. Cold water. The smell of smoke filled my nose. I winced as I felt a massive headache start to form. Straining my smoke-filled eyes, I searched for my horse, but she was nowhere in sight. I scrambled to my feet, groaning as I did so. How long had I laid in the creek? I picked my sword up from the ground where it had fallen from my hand when I slipped. My arrows were scattered on the ground. I picked them up and put them in my quiver. Miraculously, my bow was still intact. But where was the string? I searched the ground, caught sight of it, and walked over to it.

As I bent to pick it up, a streak of silver flew over my head, burying itself into a tree behind me. I faced where I thought the person who had thrown the dagger was. Miryant sighed as he stepped from the woods. I stared at him. I had assumed the dragon fire had gotten him, but maybe he had been too far away from it.

He smiled at my shocked expression and said, "We meet again, so soon too. What a pleasure. Now, I will try to make this as simple as possible. You know what the Code of Kings is, correct?"

I blinked, trying to think clearly. It dawned on me what he was saying and I replied, "Of course, why?"

"You are then familiar with the part that says if a royal or noble challenges another noble or royal to a sword fight, that person must accept or be considered a disgrace." I did not like where this was going.

"Yes, I am aware of that."

"So, I challenge you, Princess Arilina of Alderia, to a sword fight."

"But you are not royalty or nobility. Therefore, it is within my rights to refuse."

"On the contrary, I am the nephew of the king of Brinderia and a cousin to the prince. My blood is indeed royal, your highness."

"What a convenient story. Prove it." He untied something from around his neck and threw it to me. It was a wooden circle on a string. I flipped it over and my heart sank as I recognized the symbol of the royal house of Brinderia. He was telling the truth.

"Then we must sword fight?"

"Yes. Now we are both well aware of what happens to the loser, right?"

"Whoever loses must do what the other asks of him. But there are not any witnesses. The Code states that two or more witnesses have to be present."

"I see two people here."

"The witnesses have to be different from the people involved in the sword fight."

"And where does it say that?"

"In the—" I paused, trying to remember, then with a sinking heart I realized he was right.

He smiled at my distress. "If I win, you come with me, no attempts to escape. And what do you want if you win?"

"If I win, I go free, I take your horse, and you go back to your own country and never step foot in Alderia again." As I finished saying this, he threw his sword into the ground, so that the hilt was leaning toward him. I knew what he was doing. To accept his challenge, I had to throw my sword so they would form an X. I also knew that the goal was only to disarm the other person. I took a deep breath and, forgetting my soreness, threw the sword. It landed perfectly. We both walked up and pulled our swords out at the same time.

Chapter Five

Our swords collided. He was better at handling his sword by far, but I was quicker on my feet. He was moving his sword so fast that it was a blur. I was just barely blocking some of his faster thrusts. Like a deadly dance, we went around and around. Most of the time, I was on the defensive, but a few times he was. Sparks flew as the sound of metal against metal filled the small clearing.

As we continued to fight, I began to settle into a rhythm where I was no longer as concerned about him disarming me but more focused on winning. At last, I found my opening. I lunged forward, twirling my sword counter-clockwise and whipping it up at the same time. It was a trick that Father had taught me a long time ago. The man was caught by surprise and was not prepared for my next attack. With an expert flick of my wrist, his sword went clattering to the ground.

While he was staring at his sword hand, I darted in and slammed the hilt of my sword into his temple. He staggered for a moment, then fell to the ground. After removing his other daggers, I tied his hands behind his back with a rope. I had found it in one of his pockets, probably from the supply that he had used to tie me. A few minutes later, he groaned, sat up, and tried to touch his head with his hands. That was when he discovered that they were tied.

He looked at me and asked, "Why did you tie me up? You never said I was to be your prisoner if you won."

"You are not my prisoner. I am merely making it easier for you to keep your word about giving me your horse. To put it bluntly, I do not trust you one bit."

"Well, by making one thing easier you have made another almost impossible. I am supposed to be leaving Alderia as soon as possible, remember?"

"As soon as you tell me where your horse is, I will untie the rope and you will be able to return to Brinderia."

"In the woods over there." He gestured with his head in the general direction. After searching for ten minutes, I found the animal. I returned to where he was on the ground. I strung my bow and fitted an arrow to the string.

"What are you doing?" he asked a little concerned for the first time.

"Untying you, of course."

"With a bow?"

"No, with a knife." I unsheathed my boot blade and cut his bonds.

In one smooth motion, I dropped the knife and drew back the string. "If I can still see you in fifteen seconds I am going to fire, and if I ever see you again, there will be no mercy. Now, go!" He disappeared into the woods and I put my arrow back into the quiver. I sighed, picked up the rope I had cut off him and tied it around the horse's neck as makeshift reins. I needed to get back to Alderia. I mounted and rode until the sun set.

The next morning, I saw the landmark Twisted Trees and realized I had gone too far south. It would take me an extra day to get back to the castle. I rode hard, trying to make up for the lost time. We finally stopped at the edge of the woods just as the sun was disappearing behind the horizon.

The beautiful evening was scarred by the shouts of men and the clash of swords. I stared in horror at my home. Foreign horsemen, archers, and infantrymen were scattered outside the castle walls. We were under attack by an invading army!

"Oh, think, Arilina! Now, what? I have to get to the castle, but how...? Go to Hositela; gather your allies!" I turned back into the cover of the woods and began to head east to our nearest ally.

I had been riding for three hours when I saw torches and fire ahead of me. I slowed my pace and dismounted. I crept closer to the fire trying to figure out into whose camp I had stumbled. Suddenly my arms were grabbed from behind and a hand went over my mouth. I struggled fiercely but soon realized it was useless. When I quieted, I could hear my captors talking.

"Why, it is only a girl!"

"That does not mean she is not a spy."

"But a girl? Surely, she cannot be dangerous!"

"Remember what our captain says: 'Always be on your guard.' We have to take her to the king." They pulled me, struggling, toward an elaborate tent. Two guards stood in front of the tent, motionless.

One of my captors stepped forward and addressed the guards. "We caught this one slinking around our camp. We want to know what the king wants to be done with the spy."

A voice from inside the tent replied, "Let them in." The guards stepped aside and opened the tent flaps. We walked in and I was shoved to my knees.

"Sire! We caught a spy. What should we do with her?"

"Well, what does this girl have to say for herself?" I looked up into the face of the speaker. I recognized him, Hositela's king.

I released a sigh of relief. "Your majesty, I am no spy. I am Princess Arilina of Alderia."

Surprise flickered across his face. "How interesting. But can you prove it?"

I removed a necklace from my neck. "This is the heirloom that every princess of Alderia wears. I am who I say I am."

"But why are you outside your castle walls? Surely Alderia has not fallen so swiftly."

"Sire, I had been kidnapped and was outside the castle when the invading army attacked. I just came from there, and the invaders had yet to triumph over Alderia. I do not know how long they have been like this. I have been gone for three days now. I assume they must have attacked soon after I was captured. Either that or you have responded with breathtaking speed, sire."

"Your father sent his swiftest messengers to us and we responded as fast as we could, but they have been attacking for almost three days now."

"But why are you not attacking now? Why not take the enemy by surprise as it slumbers?"

"My men are weary from the quick march. I thought it more profitable to wait to be at our best than charge early when so many of us are tired. But I will assure you we will attack at first light."

"And me? What am I supposed to do, sire?"

"You will stay behind with the healers."

"No! I am going to war with you!"

"Your highness, you are under my authority now. If anything would happen to you, I would be the one held responsible. Please, do as I tell you. I do not want you to be hurt."

I bowed my head. "My apologies for my outburst, sire. I will do as you have said although everything in me begs to be allowed to fight. But I do understand the reason you must leave me behind."

"Thank you for understanding, Princess Arilina. You have made my heart lighter, knowing you will respect my wishes and be out of harm's way. Now, take this lady to a tent of her own. See that she has food and anything else she desires. Remember, she is a princess and my honored guest; you will treat her as such." I turned and saw the men who had caught me. They were now bowing humbly before me.

One glanced at me and said, "We are extremely sorry for accusing you of being a spy and for treating you with such rudeness, your highness."

"You did not know who I was, so your discourtesy is not held against you."

The two men led me to a tent and brought me food. After I ate, I fell into an exhausted sleep, thankful to once again sleep upon something softer than the ground.

I awoke to the sound of many people moving around outside. I stepped out of my tent and saw orderly lines of men marching off into the darkness. Desperately, I wished I could break my promise and go with them, but I stopped myself. It would be dark for another three hours, so I returned to my borrowed tent and drifted into a troubled sleep.

When I woke up again, the sun was rising; Hositela should have begun to fight. I exited the tent and looked around me. The healers were making last-minute preparations for any forthcoming injured knights;.

I approached one, a woman, and asked, "Is there anything I can do to help?"

The woman looked at me for a second before recognizing me. "Your highness," she said, curtsying. "And as for what you can do to help? Hmm. Well, promise me, you will not *ever* cause a needless war only for the sake of becoming more powerful. War is such a dreadful thing, avoid it if you can."

I finally replied, confused at what I should say. "I will do my best."

"Sometimes that is all we can do. Never forget that."

"I will not, thank you."

"Thank you for listening to the opinions of one lowly healer employed in the king's service."

"After today, many men will say you are not a lowly healer, but a lifesaver, their hero." I smiled at her and turned away, leaving the rest of the healers as well. I did not fit in here. I belonged at home in the castle with my family.

Chapter Six

"Do not be sad, pretty lady, they will win."

"What?" I looked around me, trying to find the source of the voice.

I heard a childish giggle and then the same voice saying, "Down here, silly." I glanced down and saw a girl about six years old.

"Now, what did you say?"

"I said, 'Do not be sad, pretty lady; they will win.' My father is fighting, so of course, they will win."

"My father is probably fighting too."

"Well, I do not think he is as important as mine." I had to smile at that; there were not many people more important than my father.

"Who is your father and what does he do?" I asked her.

"His name is Da, and he makes shoes. At least he makes shoes when he is not beating armies."

I could not keep back a laugh. Da was what all children called their fathers.

"What's so funny, pretty lady?"

"You would not understand. Oh, and my name is not 'pretty lady'; it is Arilina."

"Air-uh-line-uh? Pretty lady is easier to say."

"But it is not my name."

"Everyone calls me little troublemaker, but that's not my name." I laughed again.

"You are laughing again, why?"

"You, little troublemaker, you are what is funny."

"My name is *not* little troublemaker!"

"Well, that is the only name I know."

"Fine, but I am not going to tell you my real name now."

"I was just like you as a child: stubborn. I still am too."

"Your highness!" A man came up to me and bowed. "News from the war, your highness."

"Tell me everything."

"The enemy was unprepared for us to appear and were taken by surprise. The Alderians took advantage of their confusion and led a cavalry charge from the castle. Our men swept in from the opposite side. They soon saw they no longer had the advantage and so they surrendered. We have won!"

I breathed a sigh of relief. "Please, tell me, good sir, who were the attackers?"

"They were from Salogil, your highness."

"Salogil. Brinderia's ally. I wonder...."

"Wonder what, your highness?"

"Nothing, never mind." But inside my head, I was trying to fit the puzzle pieces together. Did my kidnapping have anything to do with this attack? Both had a connection to Brinderia. No, it could not be. But there were so many coincidences, so many things that just barely happened. Perhaps Father would know.

"That would work, your highness, right?"

"My apologies, I am afraid I was not listening. What would work?"

"To ride your horse to the castle. The king wanted to escort you, but he is transporting the wounded now."

"Of course. I will go at once."

The trip was short. I pushed Miryant's horse to its limits. The castle gates were open and the wounded knights from Alderia and Hositela were going inside. I hurried through the gates and dismounted inside. After unfastening the rope that I had been using as reins, I used it to tie the horse to a post nearby. I ran through several courtyards then finally got to the Keep, the castle within the castle. This was the place of last resort, where people would go if the outer wall had fallen. My home. My family was in there somewhere, hoping for my return.

I hurried to the throne room. The knights guarding the door to the room bowed and opened the door to the massive room. I entered. Father rose from his throne and threw his arms around me.

"Oh, Arilina! We thought you were gone forever! There was no sign of you when the battle started and we could not find you anywhere! Where have you been?" He squeezed me again, then dispatched a messenger to Mother, telling her I had been found.

"How did the war go?" I asked.

His smile faded. "Badly. We were unprepared for the attack. Half of my men were looking for you in the woods and were cut off from us. But that turned out alright because they joined the Hositelans." He stopped as he glimpsed my mother.

She had tears in her eyes as she embraced me. She led me to my room, switching from hugging me to scolding me. After telling me to go to sleep, she closed the door behind her.

I looked at the bed, it was inviting. The temptation was too great. I changed into a clean dress and finally sank into my bed. It was not long until my eyes closed and I slept.

The next day, I woke up to cheering. The people were celebrating the victory. I hurried downstairs and into the main courtyard. I was enjoying the songs and music when everything grew silent.

I turned to a man beside me and asked, "What are they doing? Why did everything get so quiet?"

"It is a salute to the fallen. From now on their names will be engraved on a stone under the title of 'The Salogil Attack.'

Friends, family, husbands, fathers: no one will be forgotten."

The Hositelan healer was right: war was dreadful. How many families had been torn apart by this war? How many children waited for their fathers to come home, yet they never returned? I had no desire to partake in the festivities after those thoughts. So, I returned to my room for the rest of the day plagued by thoughts of the effects of war.

Another day passed before Father could hear the story of my capture. He listened intently to it, paying attention to every detail.

When I had finished, he frowned. "It troubles me that they could so easily trick us into separating our army."

"It was a brilliant plan, but it did not work. We triumphed."

"Yes, we did, but..." he trailed off, and I knew he was thinking of the fallen.

Chapter Seven

Eight months later...

Sweat dripped from my forehead as I blocked a sword thrust. I whirled and ducked. Then, with a deliberate twist of my blade, I yanked the sword out of the young man's hand. His face filled with embarrassment as he picked up his sword and shoved it back into its sheath.

"An excellent show of sword handling, Princess Arilina. I suppose, since I, um, lost, I will leave for my kingdom tomorrow." He bowed and left.

"Safe travels," I called as I turned toward Father. I waited until the prince was gone before starting. "Father, I wish that you had made a different agreement with Mother about my suitors."

"And why is that? So far, the arrangement has worked perfectly. When I told your mother that all marriage candidates must win a sword fight with you, she quickly agreed. You bested every single one of those so-called swordsmen so far," he exclaimed.

"So far! That is the thing, Father, what if someone does beat me? I do not want to be married. Why, that man from Enlider almost beat me, Father!"

"Almost, but he did not. Arilina, I still do not understand what you are upset about. I think it is time for you to go now; I have matters to attend to."

"Yes, Father," I answered obediently, but inwardly, I seethed. He acted like I was a young girl, but my eighteenth birthday was only two weeks away. Still, there was an advantage to this arrangement. Now, at last, I could have all my weapons in plain view. The first time I had been around the village with my weaponry showing, there had been a few murmurs, but now everyone had grown accustomed to it.

I entered my room, closing the door behind me. I removed all my weapons except my personal sword, so I could have them polished and sharpened. Wearing all my weapons had been hard on them. My bowstring was beginning to fray as well. I told a servant what I wanted to have done with them and left.

After walking several paces down the hallway, I stopped. What was that? Taking a few more steps, I realized someone was following me. Cautiously, I stepped three times, whirling when I stopped. I spied the edge of someone's cloak disappearing behind a stone pillar. I crossed the hallway to the pillar and found a man behind it. He was wearing royal clothes and was almost a head taller than me.

"What are you doing in this hallway?" I inquired. "This is the royal family's private chambers!"

"Forgive me," he said, his hazel eyes apologetic. "I was looking for the throne room to talk to the king about the princess, but somehow I got lost along the way." He flashed me a smile that I am sure charmed girls from his kingdom. But, unfortunately for him, I was not charmed.

"Well, the throne room is that way, but the king will meet you in the courtyard." I threw him an irritated glare as I led him toward the courtyard. He barged into *my* castle and wandered through it to find *my* father to talk to him about *me*! Who did this man think he was? Another thought flashed through my head. What if he did not know I was the princess? It seemed possible. I was not wearing an expensive dress and he had not bowed. He had seemed bewildered when I had told him that Father would meet him in the courtyard. After all, servants did not usually know what the king did. I smiled. I could use that to my advantage to embarrass this arrogant man. Father was still in the courtyard, talking to a guard.

I called to Father, "This man is here to meet you, Father. He said it had something to do with me." I grinned when I observed the man's shocked expression.

He gained control of his features and swept into a grand bow before me. "My lady, I had no idea that you were the princess. Pray, forgive me." Turning to Father, he continued, "Your majesty, rumors have come to my kingdom saying that your daughter is now accepting suitors. I have traveled from Brinderia to see if those rumors are true." He looked up hopefully at Father when he had concluded. I rolled my eyes behind his back.

Father stood, “The rumors are true. My daughter has come of age to find a suitable companion for the rest of her life. You do seem to be a likely candidate, but I have my stipulations.”

“Name them,” the prince replied.

“You must win a sword fight.”

“Of course, who am I fighting?” he questioned as he brandished his sword.

“Me.”

Shocked, he turned to me. My sword was poised in front of me ready for his first attack.

He looked amused as if this was some child's trick. “I could not possibly fight a lady.”

My blue eyes narrowed and I gripped the sword handle until my knuckles turned white. “We will see who is amused at the end,” I muttered and swung my sword. He jumped back out of the way, and I once again resumed my first stance.

“As you wish, then.” With a slash toward me, he advanced. I knocked it away and returned it with several thrusts that he blocked just as simply. With each attack and counterattack, the fight increased in difficulty.

Just as he was about to swing his sword at me, mother's voice caught us both off-guard. “Arilina, where are you?” I recovered first and bumped his sword to the ground.

“Princess Arilina, you are the first person to ever disarm me,” he spoke in an astonished tone. He bowed again and hurried from the courtyard, heading to the stables. I had to admit that he had been a tough opponent, and it would have been nice to have learned some of his techniques.

I shook my head, getting rid of all thoughts of the man, and turned to Mother, “What did you want, Mother?”

“You chased away another suitor,” she said, ignoring my question. “Oh, Arilina, whatever will become of you?”

What would happen to me? Two hours later, I was still mulling over Mother's words. I released my next dagger, burying it into the middle of the target. The next one clanged against the daggers that were already stuck to the center, falling to the ground. I sighed and picked it up. I pulled my daggers from the target and tucked them into a belt made for the knives. Shooting my bow would make me feel better; it always did. After I had shattered one of my arrows from shooting at the same target too much, I stopped.

"So, you are an archer in addition to a swords-woman?"

I whirled around and spotted the Brinderian prince leaning against a tree. Did he not have anything better to do?

"I suppose you could say that," I answered.

"You are fascinating. Unfortunately, I must return to my kingdom, so we cannot get to know one another better."

"A pity." Sarcasm dripped from my words.

He touched his hat and bowed in another elegant bow, "Farewell, beautiful princess." I stared after his back as he walked away.

Beautiful? I walked to the pool in the middle of the courtyard and gazed in. My reflection stared back up at me. *Beautiful?* I thought again. I studied my face—I had blue eyes that I always thought were too big. I did have lovely golden hair that fell almost to my waist. My nose turned up somewhat, giving me a slightly snobbish appearance. Peering closer into the water, I discovered faint freckles. I sighed. Those freckles had come because I had forgotten to wear my hat... again. If Mother saw them, she would have a fit.

I traveled down to the stables. I stopped outside Leilia's stall and stared at the empty stall. She had never come back after she got spooked by the dragon. Either the dragon's fire or the army that encircled my home had gotten her. Whatever had happened, I now no longer had my beloved horse. I remembered the day I had gotten her, six years ago. Just a filly then, she had captured my heart. But now she was gone. Things changed so fast. I missed her dearly.

I turned away from the stall and headed toward the stalls where we kept our guests' horses. I loved going down there to study different horses. I looked for their weaknesses and strengths. I paused outside the stall of a breathtaking buckskin stallion. His brown mane and tail contrasted with his tan body. He was lighter brown around his eyes and nose, and of course, his feet, from hooves to knees, were the same brown. These were the usual markings of a buckskin, but he had a lighter tan than normal, making him unique.

"You like him?" The voice grated on my ears.

I turned to look at the prince and exclaimed through clenched teeth, "I thought you had left."

"I was just preparing to depart, but someone is standing in front of my horse's stall."

"Oh." Blushing, I stepped to the side, trying to hide my crimson face. The prince slipped into the stall and slid a bridle over the elegant horse's head.

"Easy boy," he soothed the horse as he led him from the stall.

"What is his name?" I blurted out, then regretted it because he glanced at me curiously before turning his attention back to the horse.

"His name is Leiyc."

I tried to come up with something clever to say. But after standing there, an awkward silence growing, I muttered a goodbye and fled.

I thought back to the scene. Why should I feel humiliated if I was embarrassed in front of that self-centered prince? Of all the ridiculous… I stopped myself. Just stay away from that man and you will not make a fool out of yourself. And that is exactly what I did.

Mother insisted that I say good-bye to my suitor. So, I balanced an elaborate hat, one that Mother commanded I wear every day, on my head. When he raised his hand in a wave, I regarded it with detached emotion. I swept back into the castle before he was out of sight. Only after he was gone did I realize that I did not even know his name.

Chapter Eight

The prince rode at a brisk pace back to his kingdom. The picture of the princess's retreating back was stamped in his mind. There was no doubt she was beautiful, and she was obviously skilled in sword fighting and archery. But there was something about her that was different, besides her ability with weapons. Maybe it was the way confidence wrapped itself around her or the way she carried herself—

He chided himself for thinking about her. He looked up and there was the imposing fortress that he called home. It had been a long ride, and he was glad to dismount.

Handing the reins to a page standing nearby, he scanned the walls. Not seeing the person he was looking for, he squared his shoulders and entered the castle. The damp air inside the stone palace was a sudden change from the sun-drenched autumn air outside.

Climbing the steps, he thought about how to tell his father that he had been beaten.

Two guards opened the door to the king's throne without a word. As his son entered, the king looked up from the several people surrounding him.

His booming voice filled the room. "Son, have you succeeded in getting a bride?"

"No, Father."

"And why is that? Did the king not think you worthy of his daughter? Or is there another reason?" he inquired.

"I was supposed to win a sword fight," replied the prince. He glanced at the ground in embarrassment at having to also tell his story to the people who were with his father.

"Hmm, well, I suppose that makes sense, but what happened? You are an accomplished swordsman."

"Nevertheless, I lost. My only excuse is that this was my first time facing a lady."'

"A lady!" The king jumped from his throne. "You fought a lady! But who?"

"I fought the princess," answered the prince in a tired voice.

"I heard rumors that she was gifted with a sword, but I thought they were just, well, rumors. It really is remarkable!" The monarch paced as he continued to ramble. "And she won! She must be quick with her sword to beat you, or did you let her win? No, that is not likely; you do love winning. Ah, but you must be quite worn out, and here I am going on and on. I shall see you tomorrow, so go get some rest." The king dismissed his son with a wave of his hand and turned back to the men gathered around him.

The rain sounded on the roof of my room. If there was anything I hated, it was rainy days. I could not shoot my bow, practice sword fighting, or throw daggers. The only things I could do were sew or take etiquette lessons from Mother, so I decided to sew. There was a tapestry in my room that needed mending, so I began repairing it. It was simple to fix and within half an hour I had it done. *Now, what should I do?*

My eyes fastened on my bookcase, and I walked over to it. On the lower shelves, it showed all the books Mother had given to me about manners and proper phrases for a lady. None of them had been read. My gaze traveled to the higher shelves which held the books that had been gifts from Father. Most were about dragons, swords, daggers, and bows. I selected the only one of Father's books that I had not yet read.

I settled into a chair to read it and was soon engrossed in the book. It was about dragon myths and legends. Some were true, some were not, and some had scraps of truth in them. The one story that fascinated me the most was a true tale. It was about a dragon, three hundred years previous, who had killed the king of Alderia and how the prince sought revenge. I read each page eagerly and sighed when I had finished.

Bored once more, I decided to go on a walk now that the rain had stopped. How I missed my horse at these moments! I slung my bow over my shoulder and headed out of the castle. As I passed the men guarding the gate, they stopped me.

"Princess Arilina, your father does not want you wandering about by yourself."

"Oh. Could you have guards come with me? I would like to go on a walk."

"Of course, wait here for one moment." Five minutes passed and the guards came back with two knights.

"Thank you for accompanying me, kind sirs."

"Anything for the royal family, your highness." We walked across the meadow and into the woods. A twig cracked to our left, and I glanced over just in time to see a shadow flitting from tree to tree.

"We have to get back to the castle! It is a trap!" My words were fulfilled in the next moment. Ruffians circled us. The knights drew their gleaming broadswords and I drew my sword.

The one that appeared to be their leader began to speak, "Put your swords down or the princess dies." He motioned with a hand, and one of the men drew back his bow and pointed it at me.

One of the knights jumped between me and the archer. "We will die before we let the princess into your filthy hands."

"Very well, if that is what you wish." He dropped his hand; the archer fired.

"No!" I screamed, as the knight staggered back and dropped to the ground. I rushed to his side.

Before I knew what was happening a knife was held to my neck. "Do not move, good sir, or you will endanger the princess."

The other knight glanced at me, helpless to do anything. "Your highness?"

"You must go back to the castle, tell my fath—."

"Enough of your talk!" A gag was stuffed in my mouth, stopping me from finishing my sentence. I tried to pull the gag out, but something slammed into my head and all went black.

When was the last time I had eaten? My abdomen had caved in as if trying to convince itself that it was full. My throat burned, a sign that liquid had not touched it in the past few... *Hours? Days?* I could not remember. A growl from my stomach startled me. It was like another being inside of me, demanding food. *Where was I?* I strained my ears for some clue. *Why could I only see darkness? Why had I just now noticed that? Surely I had not been so caught up in my hunger that I had ignored the fact that I was blind? Or had I?* Even with my vision gone, my attention was still on my massive appetite. *What if there was food in here somewhere?* Wherever "here" was.

I tried to feel with my hands, only to find that they were tied behind my back. *If my hands were bound and I could not see, what did that mean?* The knight... he had been shot. For me. *Had he survived?*

The gag. That was what was in my mouth. It must have been there for so long that I had grown used to it, but now that I thought about it, I felt it digging into the corners of my mouth. My memory started to come back to me about how I had been kidnapped. *Never going in those woods again.*

I closed my eyes, feeling slight alarm when nothing changed. Then suddenly I was not in the dark, the images of delicious food from many grand and glorious feasts floated in front of me. I bit my lip to keep from screaming. Somewhere in the back of my head, I had the illogical thought that if my arms were free, I could have grabbed some of the food. The urge to weep pressed down on me. I had to think.

The tips of my fingers were numb, and I tried to concentrate on the slight pain in my wrists that the ropes were giving me. It would be good to focus on anything but the intense cramps that made it feel like my insides had tied themselves in knots. A mix between a moan and a groan slipped through my lips. Oh, the misery!

Wait. On the inside of my calf, I felt something. I pressed one leg against the other; it was my boot blade. *The fools!* They had gone to all the trouble to tie me up and gag me and had left me with my knife? *Do not get ahead of yourself, Arilina. Your hands are still tied.* I bent in an awkward shape, reaching down to my boot. Something in my back protested, but inch by inch, I pushed the weapon out of its sheath. Breathing a sigh of relief, I fumbled with the blade. My hands had no feeling and I could barely hold it. Not being able to see added to my difficulty. Despite great care, I still sliced my hands along with the rope. It was not too bad, a few cuts, nothing deep. I pulled them in front of me and tried to massage life back into them. The gag came off next. I took a breath, grateful for the freedom. *Now, what? Food. No, water.*

At that moment, something opened above, and light poured on top of me. My eyes did not adjust to the burst of light before it vanished as fast as it had appeared. My ears, more sensitive since I had been relying on them, heard something drop. I picked it up; it was a piece of bread. Every bit of reason I had fled. I bit into the coarse bread, but to me it tasted like the finest pastry the castle cooks had ever prepared for me. Eyes closed, I savored the taste, the feeling of food in my mouth. Trying to pace myself I chewed it more times than necessary before swallowing. I waited for another minute before the temptation grew too strong and I ate another piece. This time the flavor faded and became bitter on my tongue. My head spun as my mouth grew numb. *What was happening?* Tiny blue dots flew in and out of my vision in a complicated dance I could not follow. With a moan, I once again lost consciousness.

ՋՋՋ

"His majesty requests you to join him in the dining room in five minutes." The Brinderian prince focused on the speaker, one of his father's servants.

"Tell him I will be there," he replied. The messenger nodded in acknowledgment and left. The prince sighed and raked his fingers through his hair. He could not get that girl out of his head! Fixing his hair, he descended the stairs. He rounded a corner and came to the dining room. Opening the door, he stepped into the room. This room was an extra wide hallway that held a long table. His father was seated at the far end. The son approached his father, fearing he was late.

But the king wore a smile and placed his hand on the prince's shoulder. "Son, you have a chance to redeem yourself. It would seem that the Alderian princess has been, well, captured."

"Captured? How?" the prince inquired, perplexed.

"No one knows for sure, but the general belief is that the kidnapper or kidnappers went west."

"I will be on my way," he answered enthusiastically. He called to a page standing nearby to saddle his horse and gather twenty able-bodied men. The men set out an hour later, facing the setting sun.

Back at the castle, the prince's father was laughing. His plan was working perfectly. Not even his son knew that it was he who had captured the princess—only his adviser knew. He only hoped that the kidnappers would do their job and not start talking to the wrong people. It did not matter if he would have to dispose of them. They were not of the best reputation anyway. Yes, everything was definitely going well.

Chapter Nine

The door or lid was thrown open again and another piece of bread was tossed to me. My hands reached for it before I could think. I dropped it quickly when I realized that it probably was drugged considering my last spell of unconsciousness. I had felt around and concluded that I was in some sort of basket by the texture of the "walls". I also had noticed slight swaying; I was moving. Every once and awhile a jerk would send me against a side.

On one such lurch, my fingers touched cool metal. My boot blade! I began hacking at the side of the basket.

⇮⇮⇮

The prince did not stop at the kingdom of Alderia. Instead, he sent his fastest rider to the Alderian king to tell him to rest assured that the Prince of Brinderia was looking for his daughter. They continued west, spreading out during the day and gathering together at night.

The prince studied the men that had gone with him. He had known all of them ever since they were small children, and they were very good friends. Each one was a strong horseback rider and well known for his sword fighting skills. A good band of friends to have if they ran into any trouble.

While the prince drifted off to sleep, his friends were arguing about who would keep watch. The prince woke up much later. Something was wrong. Why were the fires so low? The watchmen should have kept them up to scare away any animals.

His eye caught a flash of movement in the woods close by. He stared at that spot and, a few seconds later, a large wolf materialized out of the shadows. Certain that the rest of the pack lurked nearby, he yelled for his men to wake up and aid him as he grabbed his sword. Swinging his sword, he rushed toward the wolf. It snarled and leaped clear of the blade, then circled, growling, waiting for an opening.

By now, the men were sleepily reaching for swords and bows. The prince again swung at the wolf, but it dodged the blade easily. He faked to one side and it darted to the other, running into his sword, dying instantly. He heard the *twang* of a bow and a wolf to his left yelped in pain. Within a few minutes, the wolves had all fled back into the woods.

The prince turned to a man standing nearby and told him, "Gather the men, I need to talk to them." His company formed an uneven line. "Now," the prince began, glaring at each man. "Would anyone care to explain how we got into this situation?" Most of the men averted their eyes from his steady gaze. Finally, one brave man stepped forward.

"We were, um, arguing about who would take the first watch. Since, well, no one wanted to do it, we figured it was not worth it, your royal highness," he finished, not looking the prince in the eye.

"You did not think it was worth it?" The prince bit off every word. He took a deep breath to keep from exploding. "We could have been attacked by something much worse than wolves. Dragons or cutthroats could have sneaked in and killed every one of us without any opposition. It is imperative that you always have men guarding the camp!" He rubbed his temples; he had a headache now too. All of the men looked down, ashamed. "The sun is rising now, so I want to get an early start." After eating breakfast, they saddled their horses and began to search.

An hour after starting, one of the men shouted to the prince, "I found something!" The prince wheeled his horse around and galloped toward the man. He was standing on a trail made by a cart and several horses. The prince called for the other men and he was soon surrounded by the entire company.

"We will follow these tracks to whoever made them," the prince commanded. They traveled on the tracks at a canter and by midday, they came upon the cart and horses.

The material used to make the basket was thick. But after a bit of work, I was able to make a small hole. I peered through it and, after my eyes adjusted, spied several people. Noticing the scenery moving and a piece of wood at the bottom of my vision that stayed still, I realized I must be in a cart of some sort.

We were heading west, the sun setting in front of us. While the sun sank behind the horizon, I thought of a plan.

As darkness covered the entire camp, I waited until the camp slept. First, I tried the lid; it was fastened somehow. I sighed and returned to my little hole. After about an hour of cutting, I had made it big enough to squeeze out. I crept out of the basket, careful not to make a sound. I felt ridiculous holding my knife in front of me, but it was the only protection I had. I got off the cart and started to sneak over to the horses when I tripped over something. It was a man.

He jumped to his feet, drawing his sword, and cried, "Sound the alarm!" I scrambled to my feet and faced him. I did not have much time before other people arrived, so I attacked instantly. I flung myself on him. Caught by surprise, he stumbled back a few steps. I clenched my teeth and drove my knife into his arm. He cried out in pain and fell to his knees clutching his wound. I snatched the sword he dropped and turned to face the people who now were coming toward me. Torches were lit and I stood in a circle of ruffians.

Their leader stepped forward and said, "Well, well, well, the princess tried to escape! Isn't that such a quaint little idea?" I glared at him and quickly developed a plan. With one quick motion, I managed to jump behind him as I placed the sword at his throat.

I whispered into his ear, "Tell your men to give me my weapons back and to saddle a horse." The leader, with fear in his voice, commanded his men to do as I had said. Soon, I had all my weapons on a horse in front of me.

I raised my voice and spoke to all the bandits, "Remember this: I escaped from you before, I will do it again. Do not come after me, or you will feel the sting of my arrows." Still holding the sword to the leader's throat, I moved as close as I could to the horse. Then I lowered the sword and jumped onto the horse. I urged it into a gallop and disappeared from the camp into the dark of the night. We were headed east, back home. After a hard, two-hour ride, I stopped to sleep.

When I woke up, the sky was gray. I had no idea how far I had traveled with my kidnappers since I had been unconscious most of the journey. My stomach growled, reminding me that I had not eaten in a while.

I clenched my fists and muttered, "Just forget about your hunger, Arilina." I mounted the mare and readied my bow. We had gone half a mile when I heard a turkey moving on its roost. I pulled the horse up and aimed my bow. I shot and my arrow pierced the bird right where I was aiming, and it fell to the ground.

♜♜♜

Men were huddled around a small fire for the noonday meal. The prince looked down with disdain at the repulsive band. He dismounted and drew his sword. The prince moved toward the man who seemed to be in charge.

"Where is the princess?" he demanded.

"You are too late to save your precious princess."

"Too late? What do you mean?"

"The princess did not need you with your fancy clothes and your sword."

"What happened to her?"

"She escaped, wounded one of my men too."

Anxious, the prince asked, "Do you know where she is now?"

"Far from here, that is for sure. She stole one of our horses. Who knows where she is now."

"Why did you kidnap her from her home in the first place?"

There was some hesitation, and another man spoke. "We was hopin' her father would gives us a ransom for her pretty lil' head."

The prince winced at his grammar and turned away, thoroughly disgusted.

Chapter Ten

The cooked bird was delicious after my long fast and eased my hunger immensely. After finishing my meal, I mounted the mare. I was sore, as I was not used to such hard riding without rest.

I kept a steady pace until I came to a large gorge. At a glance, there did not seem to be any way to cross, and it seemed to go for a great distance in both directions. I stared at the steep walls of the canyon. I glanced down; it was a sheer rock all the way to the bottom. It was not too wide of a chasm, most likely fourteen feet across. I eyed the horse I was riding. She did not look like a jumper, but I had to try.

Then I saw it. A piece of rock jutting out from the edge of the cliff near us. It closed the gap to an easy seven-foot jump which the sturdy mare did easily. That is when I heard shouting. I looked over my shoulder and observed three riders emerging from the woods on the other side of the canyon from where I had just come.

ⳳⳳⳳ

The prince gave orders to arrest the company of kidnappers. Then he went to where the ruffians had tied their horses. Here he found a horse's hoof prints leading east.

A man ran up to him and bowing said, “All the men have been captured; what should we do now?”

“I am going to follow the princess to make sure no more harm comes to her. Tell the men to take these crooks to our country; my father will deal with them there. Oh, and tell Gaithor and Tirgol to come to me.” The man nodded and did as he was told. The two chosen men soon made their way toward their prince.

“Is there anything we can do for you, sir?” Tirgol inquired.

“Yes, both of you will accompany me to try to find the lost princess.” The prince followed the tracks, the two brothers close beside him.

It was not long until the prince caught sight of Arilina as she disappeared into the forest on the other side of a large gorge. He commanded Leiyc to jump the gorge, which he did with ease. He headed to where he had last seen the flowing cloak. Tirgol and Gaithor cantered their horses to the place where Arilina had jumped her horse. Then they too were soon over the canyon and chasing after Arilina.

I ducked to avoid a low-hanging branch. The hooves of my pursuer's mount sounded close behind me. Then I heard a *thwack* and a muffled cry as the rider ran into the branch I had just dodged.

Someone yelled, “Wait!” But I suspected a trap and ignored the plea. Suddenly, I came to a tiny clearing where the trees grew so close together that they formed a natural barrier. I looked for a way out, but the trees stood too close for us to squeeze through them. I turned to face my pursuers with my bow drawn—and was astonished to find two men along with the prince from Brinderia whom I had bested in the sword fight before my capture. I let down the arrow and bit back angry words when I saw the prince's concerned and anxious face.

He dismounted, raced to my side and asked, "Are you all right, Arilina?" I noticed he forgot to put the proper title of "Princess" before my name. His men observed this as well and exchanged looks behind his back.

Seeing their glances caused me to become more aggravated, so I said, "I am fine." The prince looked crestfallen at my sharp tone, and I regretted my words. But my pride did not let me apologize. He sighed and turned back to his horse.

"We will escort you home, your highness, then be on our way," the prince explained as he swung into his saddle. I nodded and was overcome with an unexplainable desire to know his name.

"What is your name, prince?" I ventured, trying to act nonchalant and failing.

He looked at me startled but managed to say, "I am his royal highness, Prince Ithagar Haiber. I am the next heir to the throne in the thriving kingdom of Brinderia. These two brothers are Tirgol and Gaithor. They are my esquires." He gestured to each man and they dipped their heads.

We traveled for some time in silence before I asked another question. "Prince Ithagar, how long have I been gone?"

"Four days, your highness," he answered. I considered this information. We would travel faster than the band of men who had captured me. So, we should get back in three days if we set a brisk pace from dawn to nightfall each day.

When darkness closed in around us, we pitched the tents, and the prince insisted that I have his tent. Since a chilly breeze was blowing through the trees and clouds obscured the moon, I agreed.

I awoke, feeling refreshed. After fixing my hair, I exited the tent. The bright morning sun greeted me with its warm rays. Gaithor was attending to the horses when I greeted him.

He bowed and said, "Good morning, your highness." Tirgol sat by a small fire, cooking our breakfast. Ithagar was beside him, gazing at the fire. He motioned for me to come over to him. After a moment of hesitation, I joined him beside the fire. Tirgol handed me a piece of bread with some meat on it. After I was finished with it, Ithagar asked me a question.

"How did you manage to get away from your captors, Princess Arilina? And how did you get caught in the first place?"

I proceeded to tell them the story of my capture and escape.

"Your highness, you did a wonderful job of keeping your head when things went unexpectedly," Tirgol said.

"Thank you. Although, I wish I could have prevented that knight from being shot. I hope he can recover from the wound."

We sat in silence for a while, then Gaithor stood and said, "Well, if we want to get back to your castle, your highness, we should probably get ready to leave." After packing everything up, we mounted our horses and continued our journey.

We set a hard pace, and my stout horse had trouble keeping up with the rest. I realized with a pang of sorrow that Leilia would have kept the pace easily.

We slowed to a walk and I glanced at the prince, noticing that he was humming a ballad. I had heard the minstrels sing it. It was about a prince who had fallen in love with a princess. Unfortunately, the princess, Gerdia, did not love him and hated everything he did. The prince, overcome with grief, had killed himself. When Gerdia heard of this, she realized that she had loved him too, and her heart broke. From that day on, she vowed never to love again. It was a sad, almost haunting melody. If a good balladeer sang it, tears would be on everyone's faces by the time he had finished.

My attention was jerked back to reality when my horse stumbled. She regained her balance and determinedly trudged forward up the path. We were on a treacherous path, but it was the fastest route back to the castle. We crossed countless streams and rode through several patches of woods before the sun shot its last gleaming beams of light around us.

After putting up the tents, the prince volunteered his tent to me. Again, I accepted his offer gratefully. The prince slept on the ground between the two tents, selflessly refusing the brothers' tent as well, despite their insistence.

I woke up in the middle of the night. A wolf howled in the distance, and an owl hooted from a nearby tree. Everything seemed normal, and I wondered why I was awake. I turned over and pulled a blanket over me and drifted back to sleep.

Chapter Eleven

But someone else was awake, the prince. His strained nerves had felt a slight vibration through the ground where he lay. A messenger soon appeared from the woods nearby. Ithagar jumped to his feet and made his way over to the man. The courier reached into his satchel and gave him a piece of parchment rolled up and closed with the royal seal. When the message had been delivered, the man wheeled his black horse, vanishing into the shadows. The prince made his way back to where his bed was and, after uneasily looking around, unrolled the paper. He read it, casting troubled glances around him. When he had finished, he threw it into the fire. He watched as the paper charred into black fragments that floated off into the air. The prince sighed as if a great weight had been laid on him.

The next morning, Ithagar hurried everyone through preparations. He turned as I emerged from his tent. He explained to me that if we got an early start, we could maybe reach the castle by mid-afternoon. With that news in mind, I eagerly joined in the preparations, and within thirty minutes we were on our way.

As we rode, I studied the prince from under my lowered eyelashes. He had a noble face, with a square jaw. I decided that his hazel eyes were his best features. I caught myself. *Do not tell me you are falling in love with this man?!* With a jolt, I realized that it was true. I had feelings for this prince! But something was bothering me, something I had to remember, but I could not think what it was. I dismissed it. After all, it probably was nothing.

By mid-afternoon, we had almost reached the castle. Twenty minutes later, we crested a small rise, and I almost shed tears of joy as my home rose before me.

"Come, your royal highness, my father will want to reward you for escorting me home."

"Of course, your highness. We shall accompany you to the castle." We hurried over the meadow to the castle. I could not wait to see my father again. The events of the past couple of days had been draining, and I wanted to speak to my father about why this had happened. I had a strange feeling that both kidnappings were connected in some way.

When we reached the main gate, two guards challenged us but bowed when they recognized me. They opened the great double gates, the hinges creaking under the immense weight of the doors. Feeling the horse spook under me, I soothed her with a calming hand. Still trembling, she crept through the large archway.

We made our way to the Keep. After dismounting at the first courtyard, we gave our horses to the grooms who had rushed out to meet us. With my three escorts following, I hurried to the throne room. The two guards outside the room opened the doors.

All this brought back memories of the last time I had returned home eight months ago. I entered the room and saw Father on his throne, staring off into the distance, a sad look on his face.

When he saw me, his face changed completely and he said, "Arilina! You are home! I have been searching everywhere for you! But who are these men?"

"Father, these are my escorts. You may remember Prince Ithagar; he was recently here as my suitor. The others are his esquires."

My father turned to Ithagar and said, "I am forever in debt to you for saving my daughter, Prince Ithagar."

"Actually, she saved herself, your majesty. We merely escorted her home after we caught up with her," Ithagar replied.

"I think there is a story to be told about that, but perhaps at a different time. Now, my good sirs, about your reward."

"There is no need for a reward, your majesty. It was our pleasure to accompany the princess home."

"Very well. But I do insist you stay overnight before you start your journey back to Brinderia."

"We accept your gracious offer, your majesty." Father told a servant to take them to their rooms, and after they had bowed, the servant led them out of the room.

Now that we were alone, Father threw his arms around me. "I was so worried when the two knights returned without you."

"The one knight. He took an arrow intended for me, is he alright?"

"His armor took much of the force, but he was still wounded. He is improving though. The healers expect him to make a complete recovery."

"I want to see him, to thank him."

"Of course."

"But, Father, why does this keep happening? Ambushed in the woods, again? I used to play there as a child, and nothing ever happened. People go in and out every day and nothing happens."

"Arilina, you are the princess. You are constantly in danger. As your eighteenth birthday draws near, that danger becomes even more apparent."

I sighed. I knew he was referring to the time when I would be announced as the official heir to the throne: my coronation. When I had been captured, I had forgotten about it. Now my birthday was only a week away, and the ceremony would take place a day after that. When I would become the heir, it seemed as if great responsibility would rest on my shoulders.

"So, how did you escape?"

I took my time telling my story, as all good storytellers should. When I had concluded my narration, Father was deep in thought.

In a grave voice, he said, "When you become the official Princess of Alderia, you will have more guards. This added protection will make it less likely for this to happen again. And Prince Ithagar escorted you home? Interesting, very interesting."

"Oh, and I wanted to ask you a question. I keep trying to remember something about the prince, and I think it is important. But I just can't remember."

"Well, my advice to you is to retrace your steps, so to speak. Start on the first day you met Ithagar and go through all the events that concern him up to the present."

“Thank you, Father. I hope it works.”

“Tell me if you figure it out,” he said with a kind smile. “Now, Arilina, tell me the truth, do you approve of this Prince Ithagar?”

Hesitantly, I answered, “Yes, I suppose I do have some feelings for the prince. I do not know, everything is so—” I paused. “—mixed up.”

“I know it is confusing, but if you do like him, then my suggestion to you is a rematch. After all, it was your mother’s interruption that helped you win.” He said with a smile.

“I do not know. It is all so confusing.”

“After the ceremony, tell me your answer. If it is yes, I will send a message to him.”

“Did Mother happen to mention anything about the ceremony?”

“Well, let me see. She did mention an elaborate gown, an immense party, and a huge responsibility, or something like that.”

I groaned in response as I turned to leave.

Chapter Twelve

The next morning, Ithagar and his men prepared to leave.

"Goodbye, your royal highness," I said, curtsying.

"Until we meet again, Princess Arilina." Ithagar bowed, then mounted his horse and was about to start riding away.

"Wait!" I called.

He stopped his mount and turned to face me. "What is it?"

"My apologies for being so much like Gerdia." *What had made me say that?* Confusion flitted across his face. He was about to say something, then stopped, dipped his head and left.

⁂

The prince was mulling over Arilina's last words. What had she meant when she had said Gerdia? His thoughts flew back to the ballad concerning the princess by the same name and everything clicked inside him. How he dreaded talking to his father again! The message on the parchment he had received flashed before his eyes; he shut them, trying to forget the words. But words still appeared: *last chance*, *trick*, *marriage*, *trap*, *worthless*, *disown*. He clenched his teeth and concentrated on something else. But all too soon, he was thinking about that paper again. He imagined the way the princess's blue eyes would look if she found out the truth. He shuddered. They were angry eyes, yet they held so much hurt. But there was no way she could ever find out.

He sat up straighter in his saddle, staring at the valley before him, not seeing its beauty. All he knew, was that when he got home, there would not be a welcome. There would only be more threats.

I stared out the window. It was a gorgeous day, and here I was inside, trying on the gown I was supposed to wear for the ceremony. With a flowing white skirt that met a matching bodice, it truly was a stunning dress. A lighter, filmier material made a train that attached to my shoulders. I would also wear matching white gloves and boots that came to my knees. Tradition said that the prince or princess was always dressed in white. It symbolized a fresh start. My hair would be curled and piled onto my head with several curls cascading down to my shoulders. When Mother had finished, even I had to admit that it looked splendid.

The instant Mother told me I could go, I did. I changed my dress and hurried to the archery range. The tension fell off me as I shot my bow. It was so enjoyable to hear the arrows hit the target with a satisfying *thud.* I kept shooting for another hour. My shots soon became more scattered because I could no longer hold my bow steady, so I stopped.

When I had finished, Father's advice from the other day came back to me. Start on the first day you met Ithagar and go through all the events that concern him up to the present. Maybe it was not so important. I had forgotten about it for an entire day but maybe that was due to the several blows to the head I had received recently. Still, I wanted to figure it out. As I walked back to my room, I replayed the events of the first day I had met Ithagar. First, I had beat that other prince in a sword fight. Then, Father dismissed me, so I had gone back to my room.

Then what? Oh, that is when I had caught Prince Ithagar in the hall. But why was he in that hall? He had tried to hide when I had seen him first. Why would he hide? Maybe it was not a big deal… but why had he tried? The questions spun around in my head. What had he said when I had found him? That he was looking for the throne room to talk to Father about me, but somehow he had gotten lost along the way? I remembered how he had looked when I surprised him, his nervous smile and his eyes showing a tiny bit of fear.

All of this still did not make any sense. I continued to think of the following events. The next time I had seen him was at the archery range. Visitors were not usually allowed there, but some exceptions were made. But my thoughts turned back to the first time I had met him. There was still something I was missing.

Aha! Something white had fluttered to the ground when I had pulled him from his hiding spot. I hurried to the hallway and carefully considered which pillar he had been behind. Choosing one, I searched around it. I was about to go to the next one when something caught my eye that was stuck underneath the base of the great stone pillar. I slid out a small piece of paper. Trembling with excitement, I opened it, not knowing what I would find.

⩩⩩⩩

The prince found his father waiting for him alone in the evening room.

"Are all the plans made ready?"

"Yes, Father," the prince replied. "But are you sure that we have to do this? I mean, is there not a better way? Perhaps one that does not involve so much betrayal and bloodshed of innocent, unarmed people?"

"Are you challenging what I say now, son?" thundered the king.

"All I am suggesting—" The prince was cut off by a vicious glare from the king.

The king was so different when he was with other people.

"If you are no longer with me, you are against me. Everything is ready now. I await your answer; will you go with me or not?"

Ithagar held his father's gaze and replied, "No, I will not join you in this dreadful deed."

"If that is your wish, so be it." The king motioned to the guards in the hallway. "Take him to the east tower and lock him in there."

"To hear is to obey, sire," the two guards said in unison. They each grabbed one of Ithagar's arms.

The king waved a hand, "Wait." The men stopped.

Ithagar took the time to protest. "You will not get away with this, Father! Arilina and her father will figure it out, somehow!"

The king ignored his son's words and pressed his signet ring into a lump of wax on a piece of paper. He stood and walked over to his son. Holding the document in front of Ithagar, he said, "This scroll says that the man Ithagar Haibur, once called a prince, is now nothing. I disown you. You are not my son, you coward." The king motioned for the guards to take him and they obeyed. The king spun on his heel and made his way to his throne room where his adviser was waiting. Though his adviser was younger than most, he was smart. That and the fact that he was the king's nephew made him perfect for the task of advising.

The king sank into his throne and turned to his adviser, saying, "Miryant, Ithagar is no longer with us. That fool of a son! One year of hard work and trap setting, and he ruins everything!"

"I warned you this might happen. I think he stopped pretending he liked the princess and began to love her. But since the beginning, I never thought he had the courage to kill the royal family as they slept."

"Yes, well, now we must use the second plan."

"Of course, Uncle. To hear is to obey." The king's eyes traveled to a map on a nearby table and he walked over to it.

"I am coming for you," he whispered, his hand gliding over Alderia.

ᴥᴥᴥ

When the guards seized his arms, Ithagar did not struggle, figuring it would only make things worse. They led him up to the east tower, which was the highest and most isolated structure in the castle. He climbed up the ladder to the small, high room at the top.

Despair swept over him when he heard the trapdoor being locked. Now what could he do? His own father had made him a prisoner.

He scanned the stone walls, looking, hoping for a way to escape. But all the walls appeared to be solid. He began going around the room testing every individual stone, for some chance of escape. It was no use.

Ithagar threw himself onto the small bed in hopelessness, staring at the ceiling. Seeing something, he straightened. He got up and moved the only chair over to the center of the room. Balancing on the rickety chair, he ran his hands over the wooden ceiling. There! A crack the width of a coin. He pushed on it with the edge of his fingertips, and to his surprise, it slid back without any effort. For the first time, he started to feel a little nervous about this hole in the roof of the room. Summoning his courage, he stuck his head through the opening.

Chapter Thirteen

I stared at the paper with a mixture of emotions: confusion, anger, and sadness. It read:

Everything is going well. Ithagar, you must bribe some of their guards at the archery range. Also, if you could get any information out of the servants, that would be splendid. Maids will be the most likely to talk to you. Do anything in your power to gain control over the princess and her father. Remember, no one must suspect anything is amiss.

In a state of disbelief, I slid down the pillar until I was sitting on the ground. It had been an act, all of it. Anger rose inside of me. Ithagar was a deceiver, no different than any other prince who wanted power and money. He had never cared about me—I had been a fool to believe he had any feelings for me. I stood up, a feeling of determination swelling in me. I rushed to the throne room. The guards blocked me and told me Father was busy.

"Let me in; it is very important." The guards hesitated before complying with my wishes. The doors swung into the great room and I entered. Annoyed, Father glanced at me, "Arilina, I am busy now. You have to leave."

I drew myself up and said, "Father, we need to talk. Now."

Brinderia's king paced in front of his powerful army. He stopped and gazed at the vast numbers of men gathered.

He addressed the crowds, "Today, we start our conquest to gain more of the world."

The crowd roared their approval. The men began heading toward the tunnels, which were a good distance away from Brinderia. The tunnels had been constructed in secret about six months earlier. These tunnels started in the Asfohrine forest and ended up in the Alderians' archery range. The men would sneak in under the cover of darkness. The watchmen were bribed not to sound the alarm, and the rest was simple: conquer the castle.

⩩⩩⩩

The prince looked around. It was just a smaller, dustier version of the room below him, except this room had a window. He pulled himself through the hole and stepped over to the window, trying not to stir up any dust and peered through it. All he managed to see was the army leaving, and he could hear people cheering and shouting.

He needed to get out of here now! He could reach the castle of Alderia before the army arrived if he took Leiyc within the next four hours. He lowered himself through the trapdoor into the room. Sitting on the edge of his bed, he began to think.

⩩⩩⩩

When I had told Father everything and showed him the note, we started to plan. We needed to figure out which of the guards were bribed. I suggested we switch the watchmen who guarded the archery range. Father thought that the bribed guards might send a message telling Brinderia about the change if we did it too soon. But I had to remind him that we did not know when the attack was coming and the sooner we did change the guards, the better.

A thought flashed through my head. "Father," I cried, excited. "We could add more guards to the watch."

"Yes, but that still might arouse the suspicions of the traitors."

"Oh. Well, we could come up with a reason for why we did it. Say that there is a rumor of dragons in the forest and more pairs of eyes are needed."

"I suppose; it does not sound that reasonable though. We have not seen many dragons at all in the past couple of months."

"It is the only option we have."

"You are right. Yes, I suppose that is what we must do." Father made arrangements for it to be done. We continued to think about ways to prepare the town without alerting any of the enemy's spies.

ΩΩΩ

Ithagar's father led the army toward the entrance of the underground passages. By his calculation, they should reach them in five hours. Then, it would take half an hour to get his whole army gathered at the entrance to the archery field. Once he was there, he would wait until he thought Alderia slept before his men emerged from their hiding place.

He still was not sure if he would keep the royal family alive. There was no reason to, except for the chance that some of their close allies might pay a ransom for them. *I suppose it would be best to keep them alive for now, and if no one wants to pay for them, I can kill them later,* he thought.

Turning his attention back to his army, he decided to call a halt. After all, they were already twenty minutes ahead of schedule.

After taking a brief rest, the army continued to the tunnels. They went in until the whole army was in the big cavern under the gateway to the archery range. There were ten men with picks to dig the ceiling away so they could exit. When they arrived, they had made a small hole in the roof with a wooden door covering it. Now, all there was left to do was wait.

⩩⩩⩩

The prince had only come up with one idea, and that one would not work. Just then, the trapdoor moved, and a plate of food was slid into the room and the opening was again shut.

He began to eat the delightful food, starting with one of the buns. But, instead of the softness he expected, he bit into something hard. Pulling the shiny piece of metal out of the bread, he realized it was a key.

His meal forgotten, he walked over to the trapdoor and slid the key into the lock and the door unlocked with a satisfying click. Ithagar pulled the trap door up by a ring in the center of it. He paused, turned, grabbed another bun from his plate and slid through the door.

The knight on guard was sitting down, eating his dinner. With a cry, he jumped to his feet and rushed over to him. Fortunately, Ithagar had been left with his sword and he now drew it. The knight stopped, considering the situation. Ithagar did not wait for him to make up his mind. He dodged to the right and the soldier fell for the fake. Ithagar slipped by him and with his hilt dealt a heavy blow to the man's unprotected head. He fell in a heap and lay there as if sleeping. Ithagar pushed open the door at the end of the hall.

A maid stood there, watching the whole thing. "I knew you would find the key." She smiled and curtsied. "Follow me, your royal highness." Ithagar walked after her as she led him to a courtyard. Leiyc was waiting, already saddled and bridled. She handed him Leiyc's reins and said, "May your mount take you where you need to go with speed and safety."

"Thank you… for everything." He took the reins from her and swung into his saddle, urging the horse forward at the same time.

Chapter Fourteen

"It makes no sense!" Father exclaimed. "Why would they think they could get their army in the castle without alerting the other watchmen?"

"I think," I began. "We should go to the archery field and see what we can find."

"Hmm, maybe, you should just go. I have to oversee the preparations here," he said. I agreed and left for the archery field.

Three other knights were there when I arrived, so I started shooting into the nearest target. The knights bowed when they saw me and returned to shooting. I barely kept my impatience from showing as we all shot round after round.

One of the knights said to his companions, "That is enough practice for today." Turning to me he bowed and said, "Good day to you, Princess Arilina." I nodded, and as they were leaving, I shot one final volley of arrows and retrieved them. By that time, the knights had gone. I rubbed one of my shoulders; there was no doubt that I was going to be sore after all that practice.

Forgetting my coming stiffness, I sped to the archway that led to the outside. There was a large meadow beside the castle and the nearest cover was the Asfohrine Forest. Father was right about not understanding their plan. There was no way anyone could come across that piece of land without being spotted. How could we protect the people if we did not know how to stop the enemy army from entering?

My eyes caught movement. I tensed and turned my head slightly so I could see better. It was only a rabbit, popping up from its underground burrow. I gazed at it for a few seconds before it dawned on me.

"That's it! That is how they are going to get in!" I exclaimed, startling the bunny, so it scurried back into its hole. I needed to get to Father! I ran out of the archery range. Breathless, I raced up the steps to where Father was standing with another man. When he saw me, he ended his conversation with the young man.

"Arilina, have you found out anything?"

"Yes, Father, I have. I had this idea that the only way they could approach the castle unseen was by going underground! They must have constructed tunnels without our knowing. I think that the tunnels must start in the woods across the meadow."

"I suppose that is the best logical explanation at this point. I am not sure how they managed to do it without our knowledge, but I suppose it could have happened."

"But now what? What are we going to do now that we think we know where they are coming from?"

"I will take care of it, Arilina."

"Of course, Father." I began to descend the stairs. Before he disappeared from my view, I saw him beckon to a man from a different hallway. I continued down the steps feeling a little hurt that I had been dismissed. But I knew it was probably for the best anyway.

My thoughts drifted to the traitorous Ithagar, and I clenched and unclenched my fists. If I ever saw him again... But still, I was heartbroken by his betrayal. Something told me that if he did come back, I would rush into his arms like I did not know about his treachery.

I took a deep breath. *No!* That would not happen. I would not be his pawn ever again, even if he denied his part in the attack, I would never believe him. I hurried to my room and flung open my closet door. The last rays of light shone on something metallic in the back of the closet. I squared my shoulders. It was time to act.

Miryant turned to his uncle. "I believe we should check the position of the sun now." Without a word of reply, the king gestured for a man to check. The man inched the door up and did a quick scan before sliding back into the dark cave. The king glanced at him impatiently. The man brushed himself off and knelt before the king.

"Your majesty," he began, "The sun has set, shall we begin now?"

“Why so hasty?” As he spoke, the king absentmindedly played with his sword. The man gulped when the king's fingers touched the hilt. Bowing again, he scrambled away. The king laughed softly under his breath and commanded a page standing close by to light the hour candle. The candle would burn out in an hour, then another one would be lit. When it too burned out, it would be time to strike.

The king turned to a small table set up beside him. On it was a map spread out that was lit by a candle. He peered at it in the flickering light.

“After Alderia, I will attack her allies,” he murmured to himself. “Then I will have the most land and power in this valley and beyond!”

The prince knew that he did not have a lot of time to spare. Leiyc was bursting with energy and they covered much ground. Ithagar considered what he was going to tell Arilina and the king. If he told them that

Brinderia was attacking tonight, they might not trust him. Maybe that was a chance he was willing to take. The prince sighed. It was all so confusing, and he would have to figure it all out later. Right now, he needed to concentrate on getting there and fast.

Soon, he burst from the Asfohrine forest. He did not have much time. As the castle rose into view, he commanded Leiyc still faster. The meadow blurred beneath him as he drew nearer and nearer to the castle gates. There was someone standing in front of them. He just had time to bring Leiyc to a halt. He had to rear to avoid trampling the person. The knight reached up and placed a hand on his reins and Leiyc calmed.

Ithagar dismounted and faced the knight, saying, "I must see the King immediately!"

I pulled a suit of armor from the closet and examined it. A year ago, I had found it in a forgotten room. I had taken all the individual pieces to my room and assembled them. It had been too big for me then, but now it probably fits. Clumsily, I put it on myself.

Peering out of my room, I scanned the hallways. Seeing nobody, I started to walk, wincing at every clatter of the metal. I made it outside without anyone stopping me. I heaved a sigh of relief; I could blend in with the crowd now. Father had told the town about the threat of attack and all his knights were gathered by the archery range.

I joined the crowd of armored knights without being noticed. I gazed out over the meadow, the fading light making it difficult to do so. I saw something moving and my heart lurched. Even in the dim light, I could recognize Leiyc's distinctive markings. Ithagar was coming. Anger flamed inside of me as I saw him gallop across the field. As fast as my heavy armor allowed me, I raced to the gate he was approaching. Leiyc came barreling toward me. At the last moment, he reared, and I ducked out of the way. I moved over to the horse and grabbed the reins.

Ithagar dismounted and demanded to see the king.

Disguising my voice, I spoke, "Alderia is not accepting any visitors now."

Ithagar stepped closer to me, and I could tell he was angry and a little embarrassed. "Young man, I have important news for the royal family."

Keeping my voice low, I answered, "Oh, I am sure you think it is important, but the royal family is extremely busy at this time. We will prepare for you a room and a stall for your mount."

The prince stepped toward me in an almost threatening manner. "I am a prince and you are merely a knight. How dare you speak to me in such a way?"

I waved his remark away and replied in a deep voice, "Sometimes there is more to a person than meets the eye." With that, I began to lead Leiyc to the stables. Having met me before, he allowed me to lead him without a problem. The prince followed.

After I had taken off the bridle and saddle, I put Leiyc into a stall. I turned to the prince, removing my helmet as I cried, "You traitor!"

Chapter Fifteen

He gasped, "Arilina! But why are you—? I mean, you are supposed to be—?"

"Nice to see you again too, traitor."

"Whatever do you mean by calling me a traitor?" Ithagar questioned.

"There is an attack on my castle tonight from your kingdom, and you ask me what do *I* mean?" I exclaimed.

"But how did you—? I mean..." he trailed off as he struggled to find the right words.

"I found a piece of paper that fell off you when we first met. You know, I am surprised that you came back. I guess since you did not know we knew about the attack, you figured you would be safe. But now I need to figure out what to do with you." When I finished, I put my helmet back on, tucking my hair under it. Then I said, "Come with me." To my surprise, he followed without protest. I led him into the castle and to the throne room, where Father sat alone reading from a paper. He looked up when we entered.

When he acknowledged me, I started in a deep voice, "Sire, this is his royal highness, Prince Ithagar from Brinderia. He tried to enter the castle, but I was able to stop him."

"How interesting. Knight, what is your name?" Oh no! I thought frantically but knew that honesty was always best. I took my helmet off silently.

Surprise filled his face, but when he regained his composure, he spoke, "Arilina! I will deal with you later. Now, go to your room. Once the battle starts, that will be the safest place for you." He turned back to the prince and studied him for a minute. Finally, he spoke, and asked a strange question, "Are you willing to help us, Prince Ithagar?"

"Yes, your majesty. I was indeed aiding my father at the start, but I am now glad to say that I am no longer helping him." Something snapped inside of me; I had to leave to keep myself from bursting out with indignation. Father was so engrossed in

Ithagar that he did not notice, but I felt the prince's eyes on me.

I slipped back to my room and took off the suit of armor. Sighing, I placed the outfit on its stand in the closet. I paused before I put the helmet back because it looked dusty. I searched around my room for a piece of fabric to clean it. Finding a rag, I sat on the bed and cradled the headpiece in my lap. After several minutes of rubbing, the metal shone in the light of the candle I had lit. I set the helmet in its proper place. Just as I finished, there was a soft knocking at the door.

"Yes, come in," I replied as I adjusted the helmet to perfection. I turned around and was met by a young servant girl.

"Your highness, his majesty wants to speak to you," she curtsied when she was done speaking.

"Thank you for telling me. Did he say where?" I asked, bending down to look into her young face.

She blushed and softly answered, "Yes, your highness, the evening room." When she had finished, she curtsied again and darted out of the room. This is what I had been dreading. Even though Father encouraged me to practice things that usually only men did, he discouraged me from dressing as a man.

I made my way to the evening room. Taking a deep breath, I eased the door open. The room was lit by candles scattered throughout the room and a roaring fire at one end. Two people were seated before the blazing fire. I recognized Father, but the other man's face was in shadows and I could not tell who it was. There was an open chair in between them, and I settled into it. I glanced out of the corner of my eye at the man in darkness. I inhaled sharply as I realized the man was Prince Ithagar.

Doing my best to ignore him, I turned to Father and said, “What do you want with me, Father?”

“Well, I was hoping we could get this issue with Prince Ithagar cleared up.”

“What is there to clear up? He betrayed us and was assisting his father, who might I remind you, is attacking us this very hour!” My voice reached a feverish pitch near the end of my tirade.

"But I no longer support my father," Ithagar interjected.

"Oh, and you expect that if you say you are on our side, we will believe you?"

"Arilina!" Father's stern voice stopped me. "I believe that you should hear what Ithagar has to say and then make your decision."

"Fine." The prince told his story, working his way from the first day of planning with his father to the present.

When he had concluded his narration, I was silent, but my mind was screaming at me. Half of me wanted to believe him, but the other half insisted that he was lying. Even if the attack came tonight as he had told us, maybe it was part of the plan to make us trust him. I thought of something else then. If I trusted him and he was telling the truth, I could have my friendship with Ithagar back. But if he was lying and I believed him, there was a distinct possibility I might die along with my family and kingdom. If I did not trust him and he was truthful, the only thing I could lose was Ithagar.

I rose to my feet and said in a loud voice, "Father, I do not trust this man, and neither should you. Now, if that is all you wished to discuss with me, I see no reason for me to stay here. Farewell, Father." I stood and walked away without a backward glance at Ithagar. I could barely keep my emotions controlled. I knew that I could not go back now.

An idea came to me then. I thought through it and realized that the plan was almost completely safe, but I needed to hurry. I put my cloak around me and picked up my bow. I threw the hood over my head, casting my face into shadows. I did not want to be recognized and stopped by someone. Glancing around, I directed my steps to the highest tower. I made it to the top shortly after and scanned the surrounding ground. My eyes caught a glimmer of light. I strained my eyes and saw more light revealed. I put an arrow on the string.

The face of Brinderia's king was illuminated in the flame of the last hour candle. The flame wavered then extinguished itself in the puddle of liquid wax.

"Lanterns." The king whispered the word, but since all was silent, the whole assembly heard it. Soon lanterns began to cast a glow on the cave.

The king faced the army and spoke, "Men, now, I believe, is the time to strike. If my calculations are correct, Alderia will be caught by complete surprise. Ready yourselves, soldiers." Turning to the men with picks, he said, "Dig! Dig till the stars glow down on us!" He strapped his bejeweled sword to his side and fitted his helmet on his head.

The men swung their picks in rhythm, but they still tried to be as quiet as possible. They finally made a hole in the ceiling. Dirt rained down from the hole, but the workers continued to work. Soon, the opening was big enough for four people to go out at the same time. The king ordered his men to march up the previously made steps. They filled the archery field. But, unbeknownst to them, right outside the archery range, the Alderian force awaited.

ⅢⅢⅢ

When Arilina had turned away, Ithagar's world seemed to collapse. His father had disowned him, so he was no longer a prince. The girl that he loved had declared that she did not trust him. He was incredibly confused about what he should do. The king cleared his throat and Ithagar realized he was still sitting beside him.

"Well," began the king, "I have to check if everything is going well." The king left, and Ithagar once again sank back into the swirling black chaos in his head. Then, like a ray of light, he knew what he had to do.

Chapter Sixteen

I had fired one shot with the initial volley of arrows when something touched my shoulder. Caught off guard, I whirled around whacking the person with my bow. With a groan, Ithagar sank to the ground clutching his stomach where I had hit him. Every part of me wanted to rush to him, but I kept my distance.

I managed to say, "Are you alright?"

He smiled feebly and tried to keep the pain from his voice and face as he replied, "I will be fine in a minute or so."

"What are you doing here?" I asked with compassion, forgetting about the battle.

"I wanted to try one last time. Arilina, I have nothing to offer you. All my life servants have done the work for their prince. But I am no longer a prince. I carry a sword, but I am not a knight. I am worthless. My whole life, I have been trained to be king, and now I will not even be that. I know no other trade. Once again, I tell you I have nothing to offer, except myself. Will you trust me?" Before I could reply, a stray arrow flew through the opening next to me and pierced my leg.

I suppressed a cry by covering my mouth with a hand. The next one escaped. Every part of the arrow inside me caused intense pain. My ragged breaths caused the shaft to move, sending agony shooting through my body. To keep from screaming and making it worse, I clenched my bow until my knuckles turned white. With the care of a mother for her child, Ithagar carefully sat me down and placed his hands around the wound. Moaning, I sucked in another breath.

"Arilina." He brushed the hair away from my face in an attempt to soothe me. But the sight of blood, my blood, on his hands made me feel light-headed.

"I have to push it through," Ithagar whispered.

"What?" The word was shaky and barely intelligible.

"I can see the tip on the other side of your leg. Brinderian arrows are barbed, it will hurt worse and cause more damage if I pull it out the way it went in. Do you understand?"

Biting my lip, I moved my head in a small nod. I closed my eyes, afraid to watch. Before I did, I saw Ithagar take a deep breath. I felt the arrow move slightly, then there was a loud snap. My suffering increased tenfold and I was on the verge of losing consciousness. Like a horse fighting the saddle for the first time, I used every ounce of energy to stay awake. My eyes flickered and I saw the arrow still protruding from my leg and Ithagar leaning over it. The fletchings were gone; that was the sound I had heard. But, of course, the feathers would never pass through the wound, so he had to remove them.

"Are you ready, Arilina?"

I managed to open my mouth without crying out in pain and said, "Yes." The moment he applied pressure and began pushing, I felt it. With every half-second that passed, the torment increased until I lost my battle and slipped into the darkness that had beckoned me from the moment the arrow had hit.

My eyes fluttered open, blinking until Father's face came into focus. "What happened?"

Relief filled Father's face as he exclaimed, "Oh! My precious Arilina! You are going to be all right!"

"Sire, I have already assured you that she will be fine; in fact, she can even participate in the ceremony," said the royal healer.

"The ceremony," I mumbled, almost incoherently.

"Now, do not worry. Everything will be fine." Before Father had finished talking, I had fallen into a deep sleep.

The next time I woke up, I glanced around, feeling refreshed. I noticed Ithagar slumped in a chair sleeping. My wound felt almost completely well. But I had an idea that would change when I put weight on it. At that moment, Father entered the room, waking up Ithagar in the process.

"Are you feeling better?" my father asked, anxiously.

"I feel much better. But what happened?" Father glanced at Ithagar, who rose to his feet.

"My apologies, your majesty, I have to go. I cannot listen to it again." When he finished speaking, Ithagar left.

"What is wrong with him?"

"Arilina, his father died."

"Oh."

"Yes, I sent four men to carry him back to his land. I talked to some of the men that we captured. They were terribly misguided. I do not want to think ill of Ithagar's father, but he has been deceiving and tricking people to do his bidding. They thought we had been stealing livestock on the borders and that is why they attacked. I am sending them back to their homes with a force of my men. They were shocked I let them go. Apparently, they had been told that Alderians never keep their captives alive." Father shook his head.

"That is awful."

"Yes. But there are people in this world who will do anything to be more powerful. It is a hard thing for some people to comprehend, but it is real." We were silent as we thought about it.

Then I remembered something. "Today is my birthday, is it not?" I asked.

"Yes."

"Then tomorrow is the ceremony?"

"Well, only if you want to. The physician said that if you feel up to it, he thinks you will be fine. The wound was not as serious as we had previously thought," Father explained.

"I suppose I can do it tomorrow."

"Excellent! I will tell your mother. Sleep well, dear." Father stood and exited the room quietly. I stared at the ceiling. What if I failed? I squared my shoulders, reminding myself that I was a fighter. Taking a deep breath, I swung my legs over the bed. I gasped a little, as the wounded leg touched the ground, but after taking a few deep breaths, I regained my composure. I managed to take several steps, keeping my balance by holding onto my bed. I had one last thought before falling asleep: Tomorrow was going to be tiring.

⩩⩩⩩

Ithagar was struggling. Even though his father usually disagreed with him, Ithagar was still grieving his death. And now, Arilina was wounded, and he had a terrible sense of guilt since it was his fellow countrymen who shot the arrow.

The Alderian king had been kind enough to allow him to stay, but he did not deserve Arilina. He needed to get back to his land to help settle the unavoidable argument over who would be the next king.

After slipping out of the castle, he headed for the stables. He hurriedly saddled Leiyc and left.

⩩⩩⩩

The morning dawned bright and clear. The ceremony was going to take place in the afternoon, so I had plenty of time to prepare. Using extreme care, I was able to put my white dress on without hurting myself. A maid came in to do my hair and to help me with my boots. When she was done, she left to find someone to help me walk.

A while later, a knight helped me slowly walk to the edge of the courtyard. I studied my surroundings; Mother had done a great job decorating. Everything was white. Like snow, white rose petals were scattered on the ground.

"Your highness, do you want me to help you across the courtyard?" The knight's voice disturbed my thoughts.

"Oh, that is fine. Thank you, but I need to walk in alone."

"As you wish." The knight bowed and joined the growing crowd. This is it, I thought as I painfully hobbled in the shadows of the courtyard. I stopped so that I was in line with a path that had been decorated with flowers and ribbons. I was supposed to go down that path when Father signaled to me. Father spoke to the crowd before finally motioning to me. I slowly started down the middle of the small road, being careful not to limp. The people cheered as they caught sight of me. I smiled pleasantly at the crowd as I continued my slow walk. My leg started to hurt, but I pressed on and finally made it to where Father was standing.

When I had reached him, he began speaking again, "People of Alderia, today is the day my daughter, her highness, Princess Arilina, will become my official heir!" The people erupted in cheers again. Addressing me, he continued, "Princess Arilina, will you rule this kingdom with fairness and kindness when you are queen?"

"I will," I answered. Father picked up a gold and silver crown, inlaid with costly jewels and gently placed it upon my head. Then he said to the people, "Her royal highness, Princess Arilina, the heir of Alderia!" As the people once again began shouting, I scanned the crowd. Ithagar was not there.

Chapter Seventeen

It was worse than Ithagar had expected. The kingdom was in an uproar! Everyone was in total confusion. The king's adviser, Miryant, was the next in line. But the people were divided. Some wanted Miryant; others said they were going to choose a king themselves. Miryant was telling the people that they should avenge their dead king and he was the person who could do it. Most of the people did not trust him, though. Ithagar's return confused everyone even more. Miryant had told them that Ithagar had been disowned, so some of the people did not want Ithagar to be king simply because they did not know why he had been disinherited in the first place. Ithagar tried to stop the rumors, but there were too many of them.

As the days dragged on, it became clear that there were two candidates for the throne: Ithagar and a man called Kasik. Kasik was a nobleman who treated his servants with respect. He was somehow related to the king, but it was a distant relation. The way it looked now, Ithagar would be king because he promised peace to the chaos.

At last, the day arrived when the decision would be made. Crowds of people, from all over the kingdom, had gathered at the castle to hear the outcome. Finally, the decision was reached in the early evening. Everyone seemed to hold their breath as the spokesman appeared. He cleared his throat and then droned on about Brinderia, Kasik, and Ithagar.

Finally, he said in a loud voice, "The next distinguished ruler of our fair and beautiful kingdom will be Kasik! Most of the people believe that he is the best suited to be our king." The people cheered when they heard the decision.

Afterward, Kasik approached Ithagar. The soon-to-be king kindly offered Ithagar the chance to continue to live at the castle. Having no other place to go, Ithagar gratefully accepted. But he was in a state of shock. He had felt that there was no chance that he could lose, yet he had lost.

He had planned that after he had been crowned king, he would return for Arilina. Now, he could not go back; his pride would not let him. He was the same as a beggar, other than the few coins he had and his horse, and he did not practice a trade with which to gain more money. As long as he lived in the castle, he would not be homeless, but without money or any way to get money, he would soon run out of the things he needed.

♔♔♔

I managed to walk out without help, but the instant I was out of sight of the people, the knight helped me again. The pain in my leg subsided when I was at last settled in my bed. Father entered my room ten minutes later.

Before he could speak, I began, "Father, where is Prince Ithagar? I did not see him at the coronation."

Father answered quietly, "He left last night, most likely headed back to Brinderia. There must be a lot of confusion there without a king. You know that Ithagar was disowned, do you not?"

"I had heard something about it. What happened?" I asked with curiosity.

"Well, I do not know all the details, but from what I heard, I assume Ithagar was disinherited because he disagreed with his father about the surprise attack on us."

"Oh. Then he was disowned because of me."

"I think that I will leave you alone for a while, Arilina. Make sure that you get plenty of rest." Father carefully closed the door behind him.

After several hours of hard thinking, I knew what had to be done. My long rest had done wonders for my leg, but it still ached. I was about to get out of bed when I heard a knock at the door.

"Come in," I called, hoping it was Father. To my disappointment, it was a maid that entered. She curtsied and asked, "Is there anything I can do for you, your royal highness?"

"No, thank you. Well, actually, yes. Could you ask Father to see me here, please?"

"Of course, Princess Arilina." After curtsying again, the maid left.

A little while later, Father entered the room. I told him my idea and he agreed with me but insisted that my leg be completely healed before I started on my venture. I reluctantly gave in and anxiously waited for my wound to heal.

In a couple days, I was able to put my plan into action. Borrowing my mother's horse, I rode to Brinderia accompanied by several guards. King Kasik himself welcomed me when I arrived the next day.

"Princess Arilina, I am grateful that you would visit the country that so recently attacked your home."

"I mean no disrespect, your majesty, but I have not come to merely visit your country. I have come to see Ithagar Haibur, the disowned son of your late king."

"Yes. He has taken everything very hard. But who can blame him?"

"Where is he now?"

"About this time, he is usually walking in the woods nearby. Be careful, though. Dragons and thieves lurk in the shadows. If you need a guard, I can provide one."

"Thank you for your generous offer your majesty, but this is something I need to do alone."

"Of course, your royal highness."

Swinging into my saddle, I set off to find Ithagar. The woods were not huge, but it took me forty minutes to find him. When he saw me, he looked amazed and I had to laugh at his reaction.

I dismounted and stepped over to him, saying, "You know you really should have someone with you on these walks. I hear it gets lonely and could be dangerous." The words were barely out of my mouth when suddenly five Leahid swooped down from the air and landed around us.

"Oh no!" I whispered. I drew my sword and stood back to back with Ithagar. The Leahid had the advantage of numbers, and they knew it. They tested us and soon found out that Ithagar's sword had much more sting than mine. One foolish dragon stepped too close and was met by both of our swords. Then, one took off while the other three remained to cut off our escape on foot. My horse was out of the circle of moving Leahid and there was no way to get to her.

The flying dragon attempted to attack us from above, but fell to the ground when I sliced its wing. Another took its place in the sky and the wounded one joined the walking ones. Ithagar managed to avoid the poisonous claws and pierce its heart. While he was busy with the one that took its place, the two other remaining Leahid charged. We both ducked to avoid the one in the air and I attempted to slash a wing again, but my sword caught in the tough flesh and was flung far out of reach. I stood up to see the dragons rallying and all three rushing toward us.

I had just enough time to warn Ithagar and run to a tree nearby and climb it. Ithagar was left alone. He had enough time to prepare himself before they attacked. From my perch in the tree, it looked like Ithagar was sure to lose. But he had been a prince, trained by the best in sword fighting. One dragon backed off, holding an injured leg high. It took a few seconds before it unfurled its wings and attacked from the air.

All in all, I was perfectly useless, shouting instructions that came a second too late. The battle wore on. If a Leahid was injured in the air, it continued on the ground; if it was wounded on the ground, it took to the air. Just as Ithagar's strength was starting to give out, he plunged his sword into the last one. He was gasping from his exertion, and he immediately sat down on a fallen log nearby, until he remembered I was still up in the tree.

Before Ithagar could help me down, I gracefully slid down the tree, landing with a *thud* at the bottom. I hurried over to where he was still sitting, trying to catch his breath.

"Ithagar, you saved my life! Thank you from the bottom of my heart!" I exclaimed when I had reached him.

"How did you know I was here? And why are you here?" Ithagar finally managed to say.

"It is simple—Kasik told me where you usually are, and I came looking for you."

"But why were you trying to find me? But first, wait… I have to tell you something. The people chose someone to be king in my place. I have nothing now."

"I know, but what does that have to do with me looking for you?"

Ithagar was caught off guard by my response, and it took him several seconds to compose himself. "Well, I, um, thought you might like to know."

"It does not matter, Ithagar. You do not love people for their position, their wealth, or their beauty. One day, none of that will matter anymore. You love someone for their character, their morals, and their virtues."

"Love?" Ithagar asked.

"Yes, love. I do not love you just because you could become king, or that you have wealth. I love you because you are you, and no one can change that except yourself. So, let me ask you a question, do you want to sword fight?"

"What?"

"If you will remember, the first time we met you were supposed to beat me in a sword fight for my hand in marriage. Now, I am asking for a rematch." When I was done talking, I fetched my sword and held it out in the challenge.

"Well, if you are sure. Ready?" he inquired as he unsheathed his sword.

"Ready," I answered. Once again, our swords clashed together. I soon realized the only reason I had won the last time was because of Mother's interruption. Even tired from his fight with the dragons, he was by far the better swordsman. It was with a clever twist of his sword that Ithagar flipped my sword out of my hand. He looked at me smugly.

I mimicked what he had said when I had disarmed him. "Prince Ithagar, you are the first person to ever disarm me."

"I suppose we are even now."

"I suppose so. Come, we should go back to the castle. My horse can carry the two of us."

We began to talk. The distrust was gone, replaced by love. We came out of the forest just as the sun was setting.

And now, like all stories that begin with *once upon a time*, this one too ends with...

...and they lived

happily ever after.

Glossary of Terms

People

Arilina Eral	Air-line-uh Er-ale
Tirgol	Tir-gull
Gaithor	Ga-thor
Ithagar Haiber	Ith-a-gar Hay-i-burr
Gerdia	Grr-de-uh
Miryant	Mere-ee-ant
Kasik	Kay-sick

Dragons

Erif	Er-if
Fika	Fi-ka
Pegerif	Peg-er-if
Leahid	Lee-hid
Leawif	Lee-whiff
Leviathan	Luh-vie-a-thon

Horses

Leilia	Lee-la
Lialei	La-lee
Eriyc	Air-e-ick
Leiyc	Lee-ick

Places

Alderia	Awl-dir-ee-uh
Etimon	Ee-tea-mon
Enlider	In-lid-er
Brinderia	Brin-deer-ee-uh
Dolemeer	Dull-ee-mere
Rasania	Ra-sane-ee-uh
Hositela	Hoe-sit-ee-la
Salogil	Sal-o-gill
Asfohrine	As-foe-rine

Made in the USA
Middletown, DE
02 January 2021

30521335R00104